Echoes in the Vale

Echoes in the Vale

The future forgot her. The past won't let her go.

Mark Harrington

Disclaimer

Echoes in the Vale is a work of fiction intended for middle-grade readers. All characters, locations, organizations, and events depicted in this book are fictional. Any resemblance to real persons, living or dead, or to actual events or places is purely coincidental.

This story contains elements of mystery, suspense, and adventure presented in an age-appropriate manner. The situations and choices made by characters are part of a fictional narrative and should not be interpreted as real-world guidance or instruction.

Table of Contents

DEDICATION

For Molly — my favorite daughter.

Remember: stay unpredictable, trust your instincts,
and never underestimate the power of good Wi-Fi and bad
dad jokes.

The Force — and your old man — will always have your back.

I wasn't supposed to survive their experiment.
I wasn't supposed to matter.
But I did.
They built a machine to rewrite the past.
I proved the future still had a choice.
~Cristine

PROLOGUE — Observation Complete

The lab was never quiet.

Machines hummed day and night, filling the room with a low, steady sound. Thick cables ran along the walls like metal vines. Cold air blew from vents near the floor, and the sharp smell of metal burned in Dr. Lena Halden's nose.

A monitor beeped every few seconds.

Beep.

Beep.

Beep.

Dr. Halden adjusted the microphone clipped to her collar. Her fingers were shaking, even though she tried to keep them steady.

"Observation Room Four-B," she said. "Test cycle seven. Subject C.V. is stable."

Her reflection stared back at her from the glass wall in front of her. Not just one reflection—many. The glass split her image into pieces, each one slightly off from the others. The overhead lights flickered, making her face look pale and tired.

On the other side of the glass sat a girl.

She couldn't have been older than ten.

The girl was barefoot, sitting in a shiny metal chair. She traced small circles on the armrest with her finger, drawing shapes in the fog her breath made. She hummed softly, a slow tune that sounded too old for someone her age.

Dr. Halden swallowed.

"Good job," she said, forcing her voice to sound calm. "Keep drawing the circles."

The girl looked up.

Her eyes were pale gray. Too calm. Too steady.

"When the clock stops," the girl asked, "that's when I get to go home, right?"

Dr. Halden froze.

Her hand hovered over the control panel.

"That's right," she said quietly. "When it stops."

Across the room, a large digital timer glowed red.

00:00:58

00:00:59

01:00:00

The numbers flickered.

Then they moved backward.

00:00:59

00:00:58

00:00:57

Dr. Halden's stomach dropped.

"No," she whispered. "Not again."

The air felt heavy, like the room was holding its breath. The glass wall trembled. Tiny drops of water shook where frost clung to the edges.

"System," Dr. Halden shouted, "halt test cycle!"

Nothing happened.

The hum of the machines grew louder, deeper, like a growl under the floor. Inside the chamber, the girl's breath fogged against the glass—and then froze in place, hanging in the air.

Every screen filled with static.

Then a voice came through the ceiling speaker.

"Observation complete, Doctor," the voice said calmly.

Agent Greaves.

"Proceed to transfer."

Dr. Halden spun toward the camera mounted above the door. A red light blinked.

"She's not ready!" she shouted. "Her brain is still developing—this will damage her!"

"Proceed."

One word. Cold. Final.

Dr. Halden slammed her hands onto the controls. "I said no!"

For one second, everything stopped.

The hum vanished. The air went still.

Then the building shook.

Red emergency lights flashed on. The timer spun wildly, numbers blurring into red streaks.

Inside the chamber, the girl began to cry.

"Dr. Halden?" she asked, her voice small. "Why is the room shaking?"

Dr. Halden hit the emergency switch. "Hold on, sweetheart!"

But it was already too late.

The Chronyx Core activated.

At the center of the chamber, a glass sphere floated between spinning metal rings. The rings turned faster and faster. The sphere glowed white—then purple—then bright blue.

Data flooded the screens.

TRANSFER INCOMPLETE

DATA ERROR

ECHO DETECTED

The girl screamed.

Her voice stretched and twisted, like it was being pulled apart. The glass darkened until Dr. Halden could only see her own terrified reflection.

"Stay with me," Dr. Halden begged. "Please—stay with me!"

A flat, mechanical voice cut through the noise.

"Observation complete. Transfer failed."

The hum died.

Smoke drifted from the floor vents.

The timer froze.

00:00:00

Inside the chamber, the girl sat still.

Her image appeared again and again in the dark glass—dozens of versions of her, each one slightly delayed. One of them turned its head when the others didn't.

Dr. Halden gasped. "Oh no…"

The girl looked straight at her.

Or maybe through her.

"Mom?" she whispered.

The word hit Dr. Halden like a punch.

She ran for the release lever.

The power shut off just before she reached it.

Metal doors slammed down with a scream. Dr. Halden pressed her hand against the glass. Her palm glowed faintly—and then faded, vanishing piece by piece.

Time stopped.

The red lights froze mid-flash. Smoke hung in the air. A drop of water hovered above the floor, refusing to fall.

Only the girl's eyes moved.

Or maybe Dr. Halden imagined it.

The girl blinked once.

Halfway.
Silence.

LOG TERMINATED — 00:00:00
SYSTEM ALERT: TRANSFER FAILED

Later...
In complete darkness, a system stirred.
A hand scrolled through broken files—metal, or maybe human. Static crackled softly. One file flickered to life.
A woman's voice trembled through the noise.
"If you're seeing this," Dr. Halden said, "time is already broken. Find her before they do."
The image dissolved.
A soft lullaby hummed for six seconds.
Then everything went dark.

CHAPTER 1 — The Rules of Normal

The first thing Cristine noticed that morning was the glitch.

She was halfway to school when the fire-safety sign on Main Street flickered. The words scrambled into a mess of strange symbols—letters twisting into shapes that didn't belong to any language she knew.

Then the sign blinked.

FIRE DANGER: MODERATE.

No one else reacted.

People walked past like nothing had happened. Cars rolled by. A dog barked somewhere down the street.

Cristine slowed her steps.

The strap of her backpack dug into her shoulder. The sign gave off a low hum she could feel through her sneakers, like a quiet vibration in the ground.

Probably just old tech, she told herself.

Still, she checked her watch.

The second hand ticked once.

Stopped.

Then jumped forward.

Cristine frowned and tapped the glass.

It jumped again.

A car horn blared behind her. She flinched and waved an apology without turning around. Her heart thumped faster as she forced herself to keep walking.

Rules of normal, she reminded herself.

Rule one: Don't stare when things act weird.
Rule two: Pretend you didn't notice.
Rule three: Keep moving.

The streetlights dimmed automatically as the sun climbed—except one. It stayed bright blue-white, buzzing like an angry insect.

Cristine passed it quickly.

By the time she reached the corner café, the world seemed to behave again.

A delivery drone zipped overhead. Two kids argued about robots. The fire-safety sign glowed its normal orange, calm and boring.

Cristine let out a slow breath.

Still, she couldn't shake the feeling that something had noticed her noticing.

She tugged her hoodie higher, nudged a pebble along the sidewalk, and whispered, half joking, half serious, "Okay, universe. Let's stay normal today."

The pebble bounced once.

Twice.

For a split second, it didn't fall.

Cristine didn't see it.

She reached school three minutes before the first bell. Just early enough to not be late. Not early enough to talk to anyone.

The front lawn sparkled with dew. The flag hung limp in the cool air. Two hover-drones floated near the doors, scanning backpacks.

Lockers slammed down the hallway. The school smelled like lemon cleaner and machine oil.

Cristine slipped through a side door and into the robotics lab—her favorite place and her unofficial homeroom.

Rose Calder was already there.

She sat on a stool surrounded by open circuit boards and loose wires. Smoke curled up from her soldering pen. Safety goggles covered her eyes, and a strand of copper wire was tangled in her ponytail.

"Morning, Mick Mars," Cristine said.

Without looking up, Rose replied, "Morning, Chewie."

Cristine smiled. "Still trying to fix the drone?"

"It's not broken," Rose muttered. "It's just confused."

She pressed a key. The drone's rotors spun, whined, and stopped.

"See?" Rose said. "Same."

Cristine dropped onto the stool beside her. "You're early."

"You're later than me," Rose said. "That's concerning."

"I walked."

"On purpose?"

Cristine shrugged. "Needed air."

Rose lowered her goggles and studied her. "You only need air when you're thinking too hard. What happened?"

Cristine hesitated. "Did you notice the fire sign on Main?"

"The one Cal hacked last year?" Rose grinned. "Did he do it again?"

"No," Cristine said. "It went backward. Like time rewound for a second."

Rose snorted. "That's just Cal being annoying."

"This felt different," Cristine said quietly. "It felt wrong."

Rose tilted her head. "You sure you didn't just blink?"

"Pretty sure."

"Then reality's buffering," Rose said with a shrug.

Cristine rolled her eyes. "You joke, but your brother once Rickrolled the whole town."

"Which is why I'm the responsible one."

The lab door banged open.

Nico Durant slid in, breathing hard. His twin sister, Lark, followed calmly behind him.

"Guess who almost got flattened by a milk truck and still made it on time?" Nico announced.

Rose didn't look up. "Guess who still doesn't get sympathy for jaywalking?"

"Harsh," Nico said, grabbing a doughnut from the teacher's desk.

Lark set her bag down beside Cristine. Her movements were neat and quiet. Her eyes took in everything.

"Morning, Cristine," Lark said softly.

"Hey."

"You passed the sign on Main," Lark said.

Cristine's stomach fluttered. "Yeah."

"It flickered," Lark said. "Like an old movie skipping."

Cristine nodded. "You didn't imagine it."

Nico waved a hand. "Guys, it's a sign. It probably sneezed."

"Yeah," Rose said, "so does the universe sometimes."

The bell rang.

Mr. Vexler appeared in the doorway, balancing coffee and a stack of papers. His tie was crooked. His hair looked like it had given up.

"Good morning, my favorite troublemakers," he said. "I can tell by the smell of solder and sugar that today will be exciting."

"Depends how you define exciting," Rose said.

"'Without explosions' is a good start," he replied.

He glanced at Cristine. "Your dad still working at Cyrex, Miss Vale?"

Cristine blinked. "Yeah. Night shift."

Something flickered in Mr. Vexler's eyes.

"Tell him hello," he said. "I used to work with the systems team. Before everything went classified."

No one asked what that meant.

"Take your seats," he said. "We'll start here today."

Desks scraped across the floor. Sunlight poured through tall windows. A half-built 3D printer hummed in the corner.

"Vale, Cristine," Mr. Vexler said.

"Here."

He paused. "You have your mother's curiosity."

Cristine's pencil froze.

Her mother's name didn't come up at school.

"Sorry," Mr. Vexler said quickly. "She was one of the smartest people I ever taught."

The printer kept humming.

Cristine tried to focus as Mr. Vexler talked about motion graphs and old inventions. Her thoughts drifted.

She doodled circles in the corner of her notebook.

Across the aisle, Rose had already taken apart her tablet. Behind her, Nico folded a quiz into a paper plane and launched it onto the desk.

"Nice throw," Mr. Vexler said. "Now try that effort on homework."

Nico grinned.

Lark wrote without looking at the page, her pen moving smoothly.

Cristine wondered what it would be like to remember everything that clearly.

When the bell rang, the room exploded with noise.

Cristine stayed seated for a moment.

Her friends laughed and packed up. The lights buzzed overhead.

Everything looked normal.

And yet, under it all, she felt it again.

A quiet pulse.

Like the world was slightly out of step.

CHAPTER 2 — The Keycard

Cristine's house always felt too quiet after dark.

Not peaceful.

Waiting.

She dropped her backpack onto the couch and stood still for a moment. The refrigerator hummed. The wall clock ticked. The air felt tight, like it was listening.

Her dad's night shifts usually meant the same thing—half-finished dinner, the news playing softly, and a note on the fridge written in thick marker:

BACK LATE — LOCK UP.

That night was no different.

Cristine poured herself a glass of water.

Then she stopped.

On the counter sat her dad's keys.

A folded newspaper.

And his Cyrex security badge.

Her stomach flipped.

The badge lay just far enough onto the counter to be noticed. Pale silver. Smooth plastic. The Cyrex logo pressed under clear glass.

Her dad never forgot his badge.

Never.

Cristine stared at it.

For a second, she thought the edges shimmered—just a faint glow, like heat rising off pavement.

Don't touch it, her brain warned.

Then another thought pushed forward.

Why is it here?

She reached out.

The moment her thumb brushed the badge, it warmed.

A soft light ran along the edge.

LEVEL THREE CLEARANCE — ACTIVE.

Cristine sucked in a breath.

Her reflection in the badge lagged behind her movement, like a mirror that was thinking before it copied her.

A knock hit the sliding door.

"Hey!"

Cristine jumped so hard she nearly dropped the badge.

Outside, Rose Calder pressed her face to the glass, rain speckling her hair and jacket. She grinned like she'd just discovered buried treasure.

"Your lights are on," Rose said. "Which means you're not doing homework."

Cristine slid the badge under a magazine and opened the door. "Do you ever knock normally?"

"No," Rose said cheerfully. "It ruins the surprise."

She stepped inside, shaking water from her sleeves. "Also, I had a feeling you were about to do something dumb."

Cristine crossed her arms. "So you came to supervise?"

"Exactly."

Rose's eyes dropped to the counter.

Her eyebrows shot up.

"No way," she whispered. "Is that a level-three Cyrex badge?"

Cristine sighed. "You're late to the lecture."

Rose leaned closer, eyes shining. "Look at the edge coding. Encrypted fibers. These things can open entire buildings."

"Or entire problems," Cristine said.

Rose grinned. "Same thing."

"I'm not using it," Cristine said quickly.

Rose tilted her head. "I didn't say you were."

She paused. "But hypothetically... what if we just walked up to the gate?"

"No."

"We wouldn't go inside."

"No."

"Pure science," Rose added. "Educational."

Cristine stared at her.

"You're bad at pretending," Cristine said.

Rose smiled. "But I'm fun."

By the time the sun dipped behind the hills, they were pedaling toward the ridge road.

The pavement still shimmered from earlier rain. Streetlights blinked on behind them one by one.

Rose's backpack rattled with tools. "Flashlight, duct tape, multitool," she listed proudly. "The holy trinity."

Cristine kept the badge deep in her hoodie pocket. It felt heavier than it should have.

The road curved upward.

At the top of the hill, the Cyrex Facility rose from the mist.

Gray domes. Tall towers. Floodlights sweeping slowly across the fence.

Cristine swallowed. "We should go home."

Rose nodded. "Absolutely."

They didn't move.

They hid their bikes near the trees. The fence buzzed faintly, thin lines of electricity running along the top.

The hum hit Cristine's chest.

The same hum she'd felt all day.

The badge pulsed once in her pocket.

Rose noticed. "Uh... did it just glow?"

Cristine pulled it out.

The light had turned blue.

"Maybe it knows where it is," Cristine said.

"Or maybe," Rose whispered, "it knows you."

A wind gust rattled the fence. Somewhere inside the compound, machines hummed in perfect rhythm.

Cristine stared at the largest dome. Its curved surface reflected the world back at her.

One Cristine.

Two.

Ten.

For a blink, one reflection moved late.

Her throat tightened.

"When the clock stops..."

The words echoed in her head.

"Cris?" Rose asked. "You okay?"

Cristine blinked hard. "Yeah. Just... weird déjà vu."

Rose nodded, not convinced. "You get that look right before strange things happen."

"Then let's not let anything happen."

Rose smiled slowly. "We're already failing."

They followed the fence until it disappeared behind a small concrete building.

A door sat at the side.

MAINTENANCE – AUTHORIZED ACCESS ONLY.

Rose snorted. "Subtle."

A keypad blinked red.

Above it, a faded sign read:

SYSTEM REBOOT IN PROGRESS — DO NOT ENTER.

Cristine shook her head. "That's a warning."

Rose crouched near the panel. "Still powered. That's not normal."

The badge warmed again.

Cristine pulled it free.

The light shifted from blue to white.

Rose sucked in a breath. "It's syncing to you."

"It shouldn't," Cristine said. "These are locked."

"Except," Rose said softly, "for people they want inside."

Cristine hesitated.

Then she lifted the badge.

A soft chime echoed in the quiet.

The keypad turned green.

The door slid open an inch.

Cold air spilled out, sharp and clean, smelling like metal and static.

"We're done," Cristine whispered.

Rose pushed the door wider. "Just one step."

Cristine groaned. "This is how scary movies start."

"Relax," Rose said. "I brought snacks."

Against her better judgment, Cristine followed her inside.

The hallway was silent.

Not empty–thick.

Their footsteps echoed too loudly. Cables hung from the ceiling. Old warning posters peeled from the walls.

OBSERVE THE SEQUENCE.

PROTECT THE TIMELINE.

TRUST THE DATA.

Rose frowned. "That's comforting."

They reached a small control room.

One monitor glowed.

Words blinked on the screen.

PROJECT: CHRONYX

DO NOT OPEN UNTIL 2124

Rose grinned. "That's dramatic."

Cristine's heart hammered. "Don't touch it."

Rose leaned closer. "You know that means open it."

Cristine's reflection shimmered on the screen.

For one second–

It didn't move.

CHAPTER 3 — The File

The hum changed.

It wasn't just sound anymore.

It felt like pressure—like the room was pushing back.

Cristine took a step away from the monitor. The air vibrated against her skin, making the tiny hairs on her arms stand up.

"Rose," she whispered. "We should leave."

Rose stood in front of the screen, her grin tight and nervous. "Just one look," she said. "I promise."

"You promised that before we came in."

Rose shrugged. "Still technically true."

Before Cristine could stop her, Rose pressed the key.

A sharp tone rang out.

The hum deepened.

Blue light spilled across the walls. Symbols raced across the screen, faster than Cristine could read.

Then the screen changed.

A woman's face appeared out of the static.

She looked tired. Her hair was pulled back. Harsh lights reflected in her eyes.

Her voice crackled through the speakers.

"If you're seeing this," the woman said, "time is already broken."

Cristine's breath caught. "Rose... what is this?"

Rose swallowed. "A recording. I think."

The image flickered.

The woman's face broke apart into blocks of static. Lines of code replaced her.

The hum grew louder.

"Turn it off," Cristine said.

"I'm trying!" Rose's fingers flew across the keyboard. The cursor didn't move.

The floor vibrated under Cristine's feet.

Metal clanged somewhere above them.

The light from the screen grew brighter—blue, then white.

"You broke reality," Cristine said, half-panicked.

"I pressed one button!" Rose shot back. "That's not fair!"

Cristine's watch buzzed.

She looked down.

12:24.

The second hand froze.

Cristine's heart raced. "Rose. The number. Two-one-two-four. It's the same."

Rose turned, eyes wide. "That's not funny."

Before Cristine could answer, the lights flickered.

Everything stopped.

Dust hung in the air. Wires froze mid-sway. Rose stood half-turned, frozen like a statue.

Cristine could still move.

Her heart thudded loudly in the silence.

Then—

Time snapped back.

Red emergency lights flashed on. Alarms screeched and cut off, screeched again.

WARNING: DATA BLEED DETECTED.

The words flashed across every screen.

Cristine grabbed the desk to stay upright. "What does that mean?"

"I don't know!" Rose yelled. "But it sounds bad!"

Sparks flew from a wall panel. The air smelled like burning metal.

The hum became a roar.

Cristine's watch filled with symbols instead of numbers—loops and spirals that hurt to look at.

At the center of the room, the light folded inward.

A glowing ball of static formed in the air.

Rose stared. "That's new."

"Back up," Cristine said.

Inside the glowing sphere, images flashed like reflections on water.

A lab.

Broken glass.

People moving backward, their actions reversing.

The woman from the screen appeared again.

"Do not let them start the transfer," she said. "If it begins before—"

The message cut off.

More screens flickered on around them. Shapes spun across them—rings, lines, patterns that looked alive.

Rose swallowed hard. "Okay. Panic mode."

Cristine pulled her hoodie over her face as heat washed over them.

The light flared.

Then—

Silence.

The hum died.

The sphere vanished.

Smoke drifted from the vents.

Cristine lowered her arm. "Rose?"

Rose stood frozen. "It stopped."

Cristine's watch blinked.

The second hand jumped backward.

On the nearest screen, one line of text remained.

TRANSFER FAILED.

SUBJECT: C.V.

Rose read it out loud. Her voice shook. "C.V...
that's—"

"Not me," Cristine said quickly. "It could be
anything."

Rose didn't look convinced.

Cristine's reflection stared back at her from the dark
screen—wide-eyed and pale.

For a second, she thought she saw another Cristine
standing behind her in the doorway.

Then the image blinked away.

Cristine grabbed Rose's sleeve. "We're leaving.
Now."

Rose nodded, flashlight shaking in her hand.

They ran.

They didn't talk much on the way home.

The wind pushed leaves across the sidewalk like
whispers. Cristine kept glancing behind them, even
though nothing followed.

At her house, she handed Rose a spare hoodie and a
toothbrush. Neither of them said how normal that felt.

They stayed in Cristine's room, lights off, too awake
to sleep.

Rose curled on the couch. Cristine sat on the bed,
staring at the dark TV screen.

"Do you think it recorded us?" Rose asked quietly.

Cristine swallowed. "I don't know."

"I don't like not knowing."

"Me either."

At some point, Cristine must have fallen asleep.

Because the next thing she knew, pale morning light sliced through the blinds.

And the world still felt wrong.

CHAPTER 4 — Fallout

Morning didn't feel like morning.

It felt restarted.

The light through Cristine's blinds was bright and sharp, like it had been turned on instead of rising naturally. Dust hung in the air, perfectly still.

Cristine lay in bed and listened.

The refrigerator hummed. Pipes clicked. The wall clock ticked.

All of it sounded slightly off—like it was arriving late.

Her eyes drifted to the digital clock on her nightstand.

7:03

7:02

7:03

She rubbed her face. "Great," she muttered. "Even time's broken."

The numbers stopped flickering.

7:03 stayed.

Like the clock had heard her.

Downstairs, the kitchen smelled like burnt toast and coffee.

The news played softly from the counter screen.

"—Cyrex Research Complex remains under temporary lockdown after a system malfunction overnight—"

Cristine froze on the stairs.

Behind her, Rose padded down in borrowed socks and Cristine's old robotics club T-shirt.

On the screen, aerial footage showed the Cyrex Facility wrapped in fog. The image bent for a split second, warping into static, then snapped back.

"—Officials report no injuries," the anchor continued. "Cyrex declined to comment—"

Cristine's dad appeared on the screen in a staff photo.

Richard Vale. Systems Engineer.

Her chest tightened.

The front door opened.

Cold air rushed in.

Her dad stepped inside.

Same jacket. Same tired posture.

But something about him felt... wrong. Like static clung to him.

"Hey, kiddo," he said.

He set his badge on the counter.

It spun once.

Then stopped face down.

Cristine swallowed. "You're home early."

"Systems went haywire," he said, rubbing his eyes. "They shut everything down."

He hesitated. "Clocks looping. Lights flickering. Never seen anything like it."

Cristine's stomach twisted.

Rose leaned quietly against the wall.

"What caused it?" Cristine asked.

"They're calling it corrupted data," he said slowly. "Something in one of the Chronyx projects—"

He stopped.

Blink.

Restarted.

"—one of the internal projects," he finished. "Above my clearance."

Chronyx.

The word echoed in Cristine's head.

Her dad forced a smile. "Don't worry. They'll fix it."

She tried to smile back.

It didn't match.

"I'm not worried," she said.

Lie.

The kitchen light flickered behind him—once, pause, twice.

She counted without meaning to.

Rose cleared her throat. "Neither of us slept much."

He glanced at Rose. "Fourteen's young for coffee."

Rose raised her mug. "Better than vaping."

He snorted and let it go.

As he walked down the hall, steam rose from his coffee cup.

Halfway up—

It stopped.

Then drifted backward.

Cristine's hand trembled.

The fog was gone by the time they reached school.

Everything looked too bright.

Across the street, two black SUVs idled near the curb.

Men in dark suits leaned against them, watching the students.

They didn't look away.

Rose muttered, "That's not creepy at all."

Cristine forced a smile. "Maybe they're selling cookies."

"Government cookies," Rose said. "With surveillance chips."

They locked their bikes and walked inside without looking back.

Every hallway light flickered once.
In order.
Like blinking.

Mr. Vexler's class felt staged.
His voice was steady, calm, like nothing was wrong.
The fluorescent lights buzzed between his words.
Cristine tried to take notes.
Her pen felt too light.
The lines wavered when she stared too long.
She glanced at the clock.
The second hand paused.
Moved backward.
Then continued.
Her breath caught.
Her pencil rolled off the desk.
Lark caught it midair and handed it back.
"You feel it too," Lark whispered.
Cristine blinked. "Feel what?"
"The air," Lark said. "Like it remembers something."
"Miss Vale?" Mr. Vexler said.
Cristine jumped. "Yes—sorry."
"You'll need focus today," he said gently.
Lark was already writing again, calm as stone.

At lunch, their table felt like an island.

Nico stirred his pudding as if testing gravity.

"So," he said, "are we pretending the black vans don't exist?"

Rose raised an eyebrow. "You're weirdly calm."

"I panic through jokes."

Cristine swallowed. "My dad said Cyrex's clocks glitched."

Rose froze. "Like... last night?"

"Worse."

Nico groaned. "Awesome. We broke time."

Lark spoke quietly. "Someone knows."

They all looked up.

One of the men from outside stood near the doors, sunglasses reflecting the cafeteria lights.

Two perfect reflections.

Their table.

Cristine's appetite vanished.

That evening, Cristine drifted through her house.

The note on the counter read:

WORKING LATE — DON'T WAIT UP.

Same words.

Different paper.

The ink was still wet.

Her watch buzzed.

Words appeared on the screen.

OBSERVATION SUBJECT C.V.
ANOMALY CONFIRMED

Her heart slammed.
Outside, every streetlight flickered.
Once.
Twice.
Then stayed on.
Waiting.

CHAPTER 5 — Static

Cristine woke to the sound of rain tapping against her window.

Tap.

Tap.

Tap.

For a moment, it felt almost calming.

Then her clock blinked.

12:24.

The numbers flickered and reset to 00:00.

Cristine stared at it until it stopped moving again. She let out a slow breath.

Her room smelled like damp clothes and metal. The corners felt darker than usual, like the light hadn't reached them yet.

Her notebook lay open on the desk.

She frowned and flipped it over.

The pages were filled with writing she didn't remember putting there.

Short phrases. Half sentences.

TRANSFER FAILED.

FIND HER BEFORE THEY DO.

The ink looked smeared, as if the words had soaked too deeply into the paper.

Cristine swallowed and turned the page.

She froze.

The words on the next page weren't written in her handwriting.

They were neat. Perfect. Printed.

SUBJECT C.V. – ANOMALY CONFIRMED.

Her heart skipped.

"What...?" she whispered.

Something clattered behind her.

Cristine spun around.

Her backpack lay open on the floor, spilling notebooks and earbuds. Lying beside them was a small black flash drive.

She didn't own a flash drive.

There was no label. No scratches. No reason for it to be there.

She picked it up carefully.

The plastic felt cold.

Then warm.

A faint blue light pulsed beneath the surface, slow and steady, like a heartbeat.

"Rose," Cristine whispered to the empty room. "You're not going to like this."

Rose's garage looked like a science experiment that had exploded and decided to stay that way.

Half-built drones hung from the ceiling. Old screens glowed faintly in the corners. A broken arcade machine leaned against the wall like a tired robot.

Posters covered every inch of space—rock bands, old movies, superheroes mid-jump. A whiteboard nearby read:

DON'T DIE

FIX THE FAN

HACK REALITY (MAYBE)

Cristine sat on a crate while Rose crouched at her workstation, surrounded by monitors and coffee mugs.

Rose plugged in the flash drive.

"Okay," she said. "Let's see if this thing is cursed."

Lines of green code poured down the screen.

Cristine leaned closer. "Anything?"

Rose frowned. "It's scrambled. No folders. No files. It's like someone crushed everything together on purpose."

The code stuttered.

Repeated.

Then glitched.

The screen flashed static before snapping back.

Rose pulled her hands away. "Nope. That's bad."

"It looped," Cristine said.

"Yeah," Rose replied slowly. "Like it's fighting itself."

The screen flickered again.

Two words appeared, glowing bright.

PROJECT CHRONYX.

Cristine felt dizzy.

"That's the same name," she whispered.

Rose nodded. "The same people. The same tech."

A second line blinked on.

ERROR: REDUNDANT VARIABLES DETECTED.

Rose stared at it. "That's us."

Cristine's chest tightened. "It thinks we shouldn't exist twice."

"Which means," Rose said, "we broke something important."

The garage door slammed open.

"Delivery!" Nico announced, holding a bag of chips.

Lark stepped in behind him, rain dripping from her hood.

"We brought snacks," Nico said. "And emotional support."

"Mostly snacks," Lark added.

Rose didn't look away from the screen. "You two always show up when things go wrong."

"That's friendship," Nico said proudly.

Lark studied the pulsing code. "It's breathing."

Rose blinked. "Okay. That officially makes it creepy."

The screen changed again.

A map appeared.

Coordinates blinked near the edge.

Cristine leaned forward. "That's outside town."

Rose nodded. "Old relay field."

Nico grinned. "Haunted place. Perfect."

Next to the coordinates, two letters flashed.

C.V.

Cristine's stomach dropped.

Before she could speak, the lights flickered.

Tools rattled.

The hum returned—low, heavy, alive.

"Uh, Cris?" Rose whispered.

"Unplug it."

"I can't."

The screen flared white.

The garage went dark.

For one long second, nothing moved.

Then Rose's flashlight clicked on.

Dust floated in the beam.

Nico swallowed. "So... we just hacked a ghost."

Lark's voice was quiet. "No. Something's still here."

Cristine felt it then—the same crawling static from Cyrex.

"It's watching us."

The flash drive pulsed once.

Deliberate.

Rose whispered, "Too late."

Far across town, in a dark room filled with screens, a man stood with his hands behind his back.

Every monitor showed the same image.

Four teenagers.

Static crawling across the feed.

"Subject located," a technician said.

The man nodded.

"Lock the signal," he said calmly.

Another screen flickered to life. A woman's face appeared in broken footage.

"If you're seeing this," the woman said, her voice shaking, "time is already broken. Find her before they do."

The man watched the screen go dark.

"Too late," he said.

That night, Cristine sat on the stairs, listening.

Her dad's voice drifted from the kitchen.

"She's fourteen," he said. "You can't just seal the file."

A pause.

"No. I won't sign off on that."

Cristine's hands clenched.

She crept back to her room before his shadow crossed the hall.

The flash drive sat on her desk.

Quiet.

Waiting.

Her phone buzzed.

Unknown number.

Cristine answered.

Static filled the line.

Then a voice.

"If you want answers," it said, "bring the drive to the old relay field."

Click.

The call ended.

Cristine stared at the phone.

Outside, thunder rolled low and slow.

Her lights flickered once.

Then held steady.

Waiting.

CHAPTER 6 — The Valk

The phone call ended before Cristine could speak.

Just one click.

No goodbye.

The words *If you want answers* kept buzzing in her head like leftover static.

Cristine sat on her bed for a moment, phone dark in her hand, heart beating too fast. Then she stood.

The Sneak-Out

Cold night air hit her face as she slipped out her window and dropped onto the wet grass.

Her bike waited under the porch light, chain quiet, tires ready. Clouds slid across the moon, turning the sky dark and shiny.

Every porch light on the street flickered once.

Like a signal.

Cristine didn't look back.

The flash drive in her hoodie pocket felt heavier than before, warm against her side.

A shape moved near the hedge.

"Don't scream," Rose whispered.

Cristine jumped anyway.

Rose stepped out of the shadows, a flashlight clenched between her teeth, backpack slung over one shoulder.

"Rule one of sneaking out," Rose said, pulling the flashlight free, "don't scare the person already committing a crime."

Cristine exhaled. "Rule two—don't hide in bushes like a horror villain."

Rose shrugged. "Fair."

Cristine narrowed her eyes. "You texted Nico and Lark."

"Define texted."

A bike rolled up the street.

Nico appeared under the streetlight, flipping a coin in the air. Lark followed, hood up, braid swinging quietly behind her.

"Nice night for illegal science," Nico said.

Cristine sighed. "You didn't have to come."

Lark's voice was calm. "You didn't ask. That's how we knew."

Rose grinned. "Group rule: nobody faces creepy time stuff alone."

Cristine mounted her bike.

They pedaled toward the hills, streetlights fading behind them. The road vibrated under her wheels, the same low hum rising into her legs.

The Relay Field

The old relay field sat at the edge of town, half swallowed by tall grass.

Once, huge satellite dishes had filled the area, sending signals across the world. Now, only rusted frames remained, bent and broken.

A tall tower rose in the center, its metal ribs cutting into the clouds.

NO TRESPASSING signs hung crooked on the fence, their paint peeling away.

The place wasn't quiet.

It pulsed.

A slow, deep hum rolled through the ground.

Lark tilted her head. "It's still listening."

They hid their bikes behind a fallen dish and moved closer.

A small terminal blinked beneath the tower.

Red.

Blue.

Red.

Cristine brushed dirt from its screen.

The logo made her chest tighten.

CYREX INDUSTRIES.

"This place shouldn't have power," she said.

Rose pulled out the flash drive. "Neither should this."

Cristine hesitated. "Rose..."

"It called you," Rose said gently. "We need answers."

Cristine nodded.

Rose plugged the drive into the terminal.

A soft chime echoed.

The light turned white.

Symbols spiraled across the screen, chasing each other faster and faster.

Cristine's heartbeat matched the rhythm.

The terminal spoke.

"Observation subject confirmed. Data sync starting."

Rose froze. "It talked."

"Unplug it!" Cristine shouted.

The ground shook.

Not like an earthquake.

Like something breathing.

The grass bent outward in perfect circles. Pale blue light spilled across the field, washing the world in color.

Cristine felt pressure in her chest, her pulse syncing to something deeper.

A sound rose—clear and beautiful, like glass ringing.

Time stopped.

Cristine's breath hung in the air.

The world held still.

Then the pulse hit.

Light shattered.

Reality stuttered.

Cristine saw her own breath frozen between heartbeats.

Then—

Headlights cut through the mist.

A black van roared up the dirt road and skidded to a stop between them and the tower.

Rose threw an arm in front of Cristine.

"Please tell me that's your ride," Nico whispered.

The driver's door slammed open.

A girl jumped down from the van.

She moved fast and steady, like she already knew how this would end.

Leather jacket. Blonde hair pulled back tight. Eyes sharp and alert.

"If you want to keep breathing," she said, "move. Now."

She tossed a small metal disk onto the terminal. It stuck with a click and began to beep.

Cristine stepped back. "It's a signal."

"Exactly," the girl said. "That's the problem."

The beeping climbed higher.

Then—
Silence.
Every light died at once.
The hum vanished.
Only the van's headlights remained.
"They'll be here in two minutes," the girl said. "Get in or stay and explain."
Rose blinked. "Explain to who?"
The girl looked straight at Cristine.
"The people who built you."
Cristine froze.
Rose whispered, "Built you?"
The girl didn't answer. She opened the van door. "Decision time."
Cristine took one breath.
Then she ran.

Inside the van, everything rattled as it sped away.
It smelled like oil and metal. Wires ran along the ceiling. Symbols glowed on the dashboard.
Nico stared. "This is the coolest van I've ever seen."
"The Valk," the girl said, slamming the door and hitting the gas.
Rose raised an eyebrow. "Looks like an old A-Team van."
"Smarter," the girl said. "And faster."

Nico leaned forward. "So... who are you?"

"Skylar," she said.

Behind them, three drones lifted into the sky, lights searching.

Lark turned. "They're following."

Skylar smiled tightly. "Good."

She twisted a dial.

The headlights bent sideways.

The world outside turned strange—colors stretching, lights splitting.

The drones' beams shattered, confused.

Cristine pressed her hand to the window. The hum filled her bones again, familiar now.

Rose whispered, "We're invisible?"

"Not invisible," Skylar said. "Just hard to agree on."

The van surged forward, swallowed by light.

Cristine caught her reflection in the glass.

For half a second—

It didn't move.

Then it caught up.

CHAPTER 7 — Pursuit

The night shattered into streaks of light.

Skylar drove like the van was part of her—every turn sharp, every move planned. Trees blurred past the windows. The road vanished beneath them.

Cristine pressed her shoulder against the cold metal wall. The hum filled her chest, buzzing through her bones. The air smelled like ozone and wet pavement.

Behind them, lights flared.

Three black drones dropped lower, their beams slicing through the dark.

"Those are definitely not delivery drones," Nico said, gripping his seat. "I'm pretty sure those are the 'bad decision' kind."

"Seat belts," Skylar said.

Rose grabbed the handle above her head. "Are those C.O.D. units?"

Skylar's jaw tightened. "Don't say their name."

Cristine swallowed.

She'd heard the letters before. Once. In her dad's office, when he thought she wasn't listening.

The van swerved hard, gravel spraying as Skylar cut onto a side road.

Rose yelped. "A little warning next time!"

"Warnings are for people who aren't chasing us," Skylar said.

Branches snapped against the windshield. The drones banked after them, lights flashing between the trees.

Cristine's thoughts raced. Speed. Distance. Angles.

The hum inside her grew louder, matching the drones' rhythm.

"Skylar," Cristine said, her voice tight. "They're tracking us through the signal."

Skylar glanced at her. "You feel that?"

Cristine nodded. "It's like... they're listening through me."

Skylar twisted another dial.

The van shuddered.

Outside, the world bent.

Street signs smeared into glowing lines. The trees stretched and snapped back, like rubber bands.

The drones' lights flickered, confused.

Nico stared out the window. "Okay, that's not normal driving."

"That's adaptive refraction," Skylar said. "The Valk bends light."

Rose's eyes went wide. "You're cloaking us."

"Not perfectly," Skylar said. "They still know we're here. They just can't agree where."

The hum rose higher, almost musical.

Cristine's ears rang. Her heart synced to the beat.

Behind them, one drone dropped lower than the others. Its light locked on.

"That one figured it out," Lark said calmly.

Skylar cursed under her breath. "Hold on."

She slammed a switch.

The van lurched.

The road ahead folded, splitting into sharp angles. Cristine gasped as gravity shifted, pressing her to the side.

The drone fired.

A pulse of white light ripped past them, tearing a glowing scar through the trees.

Nico shouted, "I really don't like lasers!"

Skylar swerved again. "Then you're going to hate what comes next."

She hit the brakes.

The van spun.

For one terrifying second, Cristine felt weightless.

Then the Valk shot backward down the road—moving the wrong direction without turning around.

Rose screamed. "WE'RE GOING BACKWARD!"

Skylar grinned. "Relative motion."

The drones overshot them, lights streaking past in confusion.

Cristine's breath came in sharp bursts. The hum inside her calmed, settling into a steady pulse.

The road straightened.

Skylar hit the gas again.

They burst onto the main highway, city lights glowing ahead like a promise.

The drones regrouped behind them.

"They're not giving up," Nico said.

"No," Skylar agreed. "They never do."

Cristine stared at her hands. Faint blue light shimmered beneath her skin—just for a second.

"Skylar," she said quietly. "What am I?"

Skylar didn't answer right away.

She took the next turn fast, tires screaming.

"You're not a thing," Skylar said finally. "You're a variable."

Cristine frowned. "That doesn't help."

Skylar met her eyes in the mirror. "It means you can change things."

Ahead, a tunnel opened through the hillside, its lights flickering.

Skylar aimed straight for it.

The drones followed.

As they plunged inside, the hum spiked one last time.

Cristine felt the world stretch thin around them.

And somewhere deep inside her, something woke up.

CHAPTER 8 — Echoes

The tunnel swallowed them.

Lights streaked past the windows in fast, broken flashes. The hum inside Cristine grew louder, pressing against her ears like a second heartbeat.

Then—silence.

Skylar burst out the other side of the tunnel and cut the engine lights. The Valk slowed and turned down a narrow service road, hidden by trees and tall rock walls.

The drones shot past the tunnel exit, lights searching the highway.

Skylar waited.

Five seconds.

Ten.

Then she let out a breath. "We're clear. For now."

Rose slumped back in her seat. "I vote we never do that again."

Nico laughed shakily. "Seconded."

Cristine didn't speak.

Her hands were still tingling.

They stopped beneath an old concrete overpass, its pillars cracked and covered in vines. Rain dripped steadily from above, tapping the roof of the van.

Skylar shut off the engine.

Without the hum of motion, the silence felt heavy.

Cristine's reflection stared back at her from the dark window.

For a second, it blinked late.

Cristine squeezed her eyes shut and opened them again.

Normal.

Probably.

Skylar turned in her seat. "Everyone okay?"

Nico nodded. "Define okay."

Rose leaned forward. "You said she's a variable. Care to explain?"

Skylar studied Cristine. "Not here."

Lark spoke quietly. "They're still listening."

Skylar's jaw tightened. "She's right."

Cristine swallowed. "Listening how?"

Skylar tapped the side of her head. "Through echoes."

Cristine frowned. "Echoes of what?"

"Of other versions," Skylar said. "Other timelines. Other outcomes."

The word sent a chill through Cristine.

"You mean... copies?" she asked.

"Not copies," Skylar said. "Reflections."

Cristine's chest felt tight. "Like the reflections in the glass."

Skylar nodded once.

Rose whispered, "That's not comforting."

Skylar reached into the console and pulled out a small device. It hummed softly, then blinked green.

"Temporary blind," she said. "We have a few minutes."

Cristine's ears rang as the hum inside her shifted.

Suddenly, the world felt louder.

Sharper.

She could hear rain hitting metal far away. She could feel the van cooling beneath her hand.

"Cris?" Rose said. "You okay?"

Cristine nodded slowly. "I can hear... everything."

Skylar watched her closely. "You're syncing."

Cristine's stomach flipped. "I don't want to sync."

"I know," Skylar said. "But you don't get to choose when it happens."

Cristine looked down at her hands.

They shimmered faintly, like heat over pavement.

Then—

A voice whispered her name.

Cristine gasped and spun around.

"Who said that?" Nico asked.

Cristine's heart pounded. "Someone did."

Lark tilted her head. "Not here."

The air in the van thickened.

Cristine felt pulled sideways—like a tug behind her eyes.

Images flashed.

The relay field—burned and empty.

The same road—but cracked and overgrown.

The van—twisted metal, abandoned.

Cristine cried out and grabbed the seat.

Skylar slammed a switch.

The shimmer vanished.

Cristine sucked in air, shaking.

"What was that?" Rose demanded.

Skylar's voice was low. "An echo."

Cristine hugged herself. "An echo of me?"

Skylar met her gaze. "Yes."

Silence filled the van.

Rain dripped steadily above them.

Nico finally spoke. "Okay. I officially hate echoes."

Skylar allowed herself a thin smile. "Good. That means you're paying attention."

Cristine stared at the dark windshield.

Somewhere out there, other versions of her were watching.

And one of them had just tried to reach her.

CHAPTER 9 — C.O.D.

Skylar didn't let them stay under the bridge for long.

"Windows up," she said. "No lights."

The Valk rolled forward slowly, tires whispering against the wet road. The overpass faded behind them, swallowed by darkness.

Cristine sat very still.

The echoes hadn't stopped completely. They had gone quiet—like footsteps on the other side of a wall.

She didn't like that better.

They reached a narrow pull-off near the river. Tall reeds bent in the wind, hissing softly. Skylar parked beneath a line of trees and shut down the engine.

"This is as safe as it gets," Skylar said.

Rose crossed her arms. "You say that a lot for someone who drives through laser fire."

Skylar ignored her and turned to Cristine. "You asked what you are."

Cristine nodded. Her mouth felt dry.

Skylar took a breath. "You're what they call a convergence point."

Nico blinked. "That sounds expensive."

"It means," Skylar said, "multiple timelines keep lining up around you."

Cristine frowned. "Because of Chronyx?"

"Because of what Chronyx did to you," Skylar corrected.

The words hit hard.

"Did," Cristine repeated. "Past tense?"

Skylar's eyes softened. Just a little. "Before you were old enough to remember."

Rose's voice was sharp. "You experimented on her?"

"Cyrex did," Skylar said. "C.O.D. cleaned it up."

Lark stiffened. "The men in the vans."

Skylar nodded. "Continuum Oversight Division."

Cristine felt cold all over.

"They watch timelines," Skylar continued. "When something breaks, they don't fix it. They erase it."

Nico swallowed. "Erase as in... delete?"

"As in people," Skylar said.

Silence pressed in.

Cristine's chest hurt. "They're coming for me."

"Yes," Skylar said. "And for anyone near you."

Rose leaned forward. "Then why are we still breathing?"

Skylar looked at Cristine. "Because you don't fully exist in one timeline."

Cristine stared at her. "That's not reassuring."

"It's the only reason you're alive," Skylar said.

The hum inside Cristine shifted, restless.

She saw flashes again—rooms she'd never been in, skies with the wrong colors, faces that felt familiar but weren't.

Cristine grabbed the edge of her seat. "Make it stop."

Skylar pulled a small device from her jacket and clipped it to the dashboard. It glowed faintly.

"Dampener," she said. "Temporary."

The echoes faded to a dull throb.

Cristine breathed easier.

"For now," Skylar added.

A low buzz filled the air.

Skylar's head snapped up. "They found us."

Across the river, lights flared.

Two drones rose from behind the trees, followed by a black SUV sliding onto the access road.

Rose hissed, "You said this place was safe."

"I said as safe as it gets," Skylar replied.

The SUV doors opened.

Three figures stepped out, moving with calm purpose. Dark jackets. Earpieces. No rush.

One of them raised a device.

The air tightened.

Cristine's vision blurred.

She heard whispers—too many voices at once.

Skylar slammed her hand on the dashboard. "Cris, focus on me!"

Cristine tried.

The world split.

She saw the river frozen solid.

Then boiling.

Then gone.

Her knees buckled.

Rose grabbed her. "Hey—stay here!"

Skylar swore and yanked a metal case from under her seat. She flipped it open and tossed something small and round toward the riverbank.

"Cover your ears!" she shouted.

The device burst with a deep, hollow thump.

The drones spiraled wildly, lights blinking out.

The SUV screeched to a stop.

Skylar didn't wait.

The Valk roared to life and tore down the road, gravel spraying behind them.

Cristine collapsed against the seat, shaking.

"They touched the signal," Skylar said grimly. "That means they know you're awake."

Cristine stared at the floor. "I don't want to be awake."

Skylar met her eyes in the mirror. "Too late."

Behind them, the river lights flickered.

Once.

Twice.

Then went dark.

CHAPTER 10 — Signal Ghosts

They didn't stop driving until the road turned narrow and rough.

Skylar cut the engine near an abandoned service station. The windows were boarded up. Weeds pushed through cracks in the pavement. A faded sign leaned sideways, its letters barely readable.

Skylar killed the lights.

For a moment, no one spoke.

Cristine hugged her arms around herself. Her skin still buzzed, like she'd brushed against a live wire.

Rose broke the silence. "So... what just happened back there?"

Skylar rubbed her temples. "C.O.D. tried to scan her."

Cristine looked up. "Scan me how?"

"By forcing your echoes to respond," Skylar said. "Like shouting into a canyon and listening for answers."

Nico frowned. "And those answers are... ghosts?"

"Signal ghosts," Skylar said. "Leftovers from timelines that didn't survive."

Cristine swallowed. "I saw things. Places that felt real."

"They were," Skylar said. "Somewhere."

The words sat heavy in the air.

Lark spoke quietly. "They weren't dead."

Skylar glanced at her. "No. Not dead. Disconnected."

Cristine's stomach twisted. "So when I hear them..."

"They're trying to find their way back," Skylar finished.

Cristine shook her head. "I didn't ask for this."

"No," Skylar agreed. "You didn't."

Skylar opened the van door and stepped outside. "We need to move, but not fast."

Rose blinked. "You just said that like it makes sense."

Skylar gave a small smile. "Speed draws attention. Stillness hides."

She reached into the back and pulled out a small projector. When she set it on the ground, it hummed softly and cast a faint blue field around the van.

"What's that?" Nico asked.

"Noise," Skylar said. "Fake signals. It confuses trackers."

Cristine stepped out into the cool air.

The night felt thicker here. Quieter. Even the insects were silent.

Then she felt it.

A pull.

Like someone tugging on her sleeve.

Cristine froze.

"Skylar," she whispered. "They're close."

Skylar's head snapped up. "How close?"

Cristine closed her eyes.

She saw shapes drifting through the dark. Not bodies—patterns. Faint outlines made of light and shadow.

"They're everywhere," Cristine said. "Like reflections without mirrors."

Rose shivered. "I officially hate this road trip."

One of the shapes drifted closer.

Cristine gasped.

A face formed—flickering, unfinished.

It looked like her.

But older.

Tired.

The ghost opened its mouth.

"Don't—" it whispered.

Then it broke apart, dissolving into static.

Cristine staggered back. "It tried to warn me."

Skylar grabbed her shoulders. "What did it say?"

Cristine shook her head. "I don't know. It didn't have time."

Lark's voice was calm but tense. "They're getting louder."

The hum surged.

Lights flickered inside the abandoned station.

Skylar swore. "C.O.D. is triangulating."

Nico's eyes widened. "Already?"

"Your echoes are broadcasting," Skylar said. "Even when you're quiet."

Cristine's chest tightened. "Then I'll shut them out."

Skylar hesitated. "That's dangerous."

Cristine met her eyes. "So is everything else."

She closed her eyes and focused.

Not on the echoes.

On herself.

Her breathing slowed.

The hum dulled.

For a moment, the world steadied.

Then—

Pain flashed behind her eyes.

Cristine cried out and dropped to her knees.

Rose rushed to her side. "Cris!"

Skylar knelt too. "You can't force it. The echoes aren't separate from you."

Cristine gasped. "Then what am I supposed to do?"

Skylar helped her stand. "Learn to listen without answering."

Cristine nodded shakily.

Headlights flared in the distance.

Skylar snapped the projector off and shoved it back into the van. "That's our cue."

They piled inside just as the first SUV crested the hill.

The Valk roared to life and tore down the road.

Cristine looked back through the rear window.

The station lights flickered.

Once.

Twice.

Then shapes stepped out of the shadows—dozens of them—watching as the van disappeared.

Signal ghosts.

Waiting.

CHAPTER 11 — The Fracture Line

Skylar took them off the main road just before dawn.

The sky was still dark blue, the sun hidden below the hills. Fog hugged the ground, curling around the trees like slow-moving smoke. The Valk rolled to a stop beside a narrow gravel path marked only by a rusted post and a crooked warning sign.

NO ACCESS

GROUND UNSTABLE

Skylar shut off the engine.

The sudden quiet felt loud.

Cristine stared out the window. The fog shifted in thin sheets, revealing jagged rock and patches of dead grass. The air outside looked... wrong. Like the ground itself couldn't decide where it belonged.

"This is it," Skylar said. "The fracture line."

Nico leaned forward. "That sounds like something you don't want to stand on."

"Correct," Skylar said. "Which is why we're being careful."

Rose pushed open the door. Cold air rushed in, sharp and wet. "Careful how?"

Skylar grabbed a flashlight and stepped out. "By watching where reality slips."

Cristine followed slowly.

The ground crunched under her shoes, but the sound echoed too long. Pebbles rolled downhill, then stopped mid-slide, hanging there for a second before dropping again.

Cristine swallowed. "Is it supposed to do that?"

"No," Skylar said. "That's why it's a fracture."

They moved down the path. The fog thinned, revealing a wide clearing split by a long crack in the earth. It wasn't deep, but it shimmered faintly, like heat rising off asphalt.

The air above it bent.

Trees on one side leaned the wrong way. On the other, shadows stretched in directions the light didn't support.

Lark stopped at the edge. "It's louder here."

Cristine felt it too.

The hum inside her chest grew stronger, pulling toward the crack like gravity.

Skylar held up a hand. "Nobody crosses the line."

Nico peered down. "What happens if you do?"

Skylar didn't answer right away. She tossed a small metal bolt toward the crack.

It hit the ground.

Rolled.

Then split.

Two identical bolts rolled in opposite directions and vanished.

Nico stepped back. "Nope. Absolutely not."

Rose whispered, "That thing just copied itself."

Skylar nodded. "Time splits here. Outcomes stack."

Cristine's head throbbed. Images flickered at the edge of her vision—herself stepping forward, herself falling, herself turning back.

She staggered.

Rose grabbed her arm. "Hey—talk to me."

Cristine squeezed her eyes shut. "Too many versions. They're all... loud."

Skylar moved closer. "That's because this place amplifies you."

Cristine opened her eyes. The crack glowed brighter now, pulsing in time with her heartbeat.

"I didn't mean to," Cristine said. "I'm not doing anything."

Skylar's voice softened. "You don't have to. The fracture responds to choice."

Nico frowned. "She hasn't chosen anything."

Skylar looked at him. "Existing is a choice here."

The ground trembled.

Dust lifted into the air and froze.

Cristine gasped as time slowed around her. A leaf hovered inches from her face, its edges shimmering.

"Cris," Rose said, her voice stretched and warped. "Stay with me."

Cristine focused on Rose's hand—warm, solid, real.

The hum eased.

The leaf dropped.

The fog rolled again.

Skylar exhaled. "Good. You anchored."

Cristine blinked. "Anchored to what?"

Skylar pointed. "People. Place. Now."

A distant whine cut through the fog.

Skylar stiffened. "Drones."

Three groups of lights appeared above the trees, sweeping the clearing.

Nico hissed, "They're early."

Skylar grabbed Cristine's shoulders. "Listen to me. The fracture line can hide you—but only if you don't fight it."

Cristine's heart raced. "I don't know how."

Skylar met her eyes. "Then copy me."

She stepped close to the crack.

Reality bent around her—but didn't break.

Cristine took a shaky breath and stepped beside her.

The hum surged.

The world split—

Then snapped tight again.

The drones' lights passed overhead without stopping.

Silence returned.

Rose let out a breath. "Okay. That was officially terrifying."

Skylar nodded once. "Welcome to the edge of time."

Cristine stared at the fracture line as it dimmed, the crack sealing like it had never been there.

But she could still feel it.

Waiting.

CHAPTER 12 — The Memory Field

They didn't speak for a long time after leaving the fracture line.

The Valk rolled through the hills as the sky slowly brightened. Pale pink light crept along the clouds, turning fog into ribbons of silver. The hum had faded, but Cristine could still feel it deep in her chest, like a bruise you only noticed when you breathed.

Skylar finally pulled off onto a dirt road lined with broken fence posts. Beyond it stretched a wide field of tall grass, flattened in places as if something heavy had pressed it down long ago.

She shut off the engine.

Birds chirped—too evenly. Too rehearsed.

"This is a memory field," Skylar said.

Nico blinked. "That sounds... emotional."

Rose squinted out the window. "It looks like a normal field."

"That's the trick," Skylar replied.

Cristine stepped out of the van.

The air smelled warm and sweet, like summer dust. The grass brushed her legs as she walked, but when she looked down, her footprints faded almost immediately.

She frowned. "Why won't it stay?"

"Because this place doesn't remember the present," Skylar said. "Only the past."

Lark crouched and ran her fingers through the grass. "It's layered."

Cristine felt it then—a gentle pull behind her eyes. Not sharp like the fracture line. Softer. Sadder.

"What kind of memories?" Cristine asked.

Skylar hesitated. "Strong ones."

Rose crossed her arms. "Define strong."

Skylar met Cristine's gaze. "The ones people try to forget."

The field shifted.

The grass rippled outward in a slow wave, even though there was no wind.

Cristine's breath caught.

The light changed.

For a moment, the field wasn't empty anymore.

A picnic table appeared, half see-through. A red blanket fluttered at its edge. Laughter echoed faintly, stretched thin like an old recording.

Cristine staggered. "I—I know this."

Rose grabbed her arm. "You do?"

Cristine nodded, heart pounding. "I've dreamed this place."

The picnic faded.

In its place stood a hospital hallway—white walls, flickering lights. The smell of cleaner burned Cristine's nose.

She gasped. "No. I don't want this one."

Skylar moved fast. "Eyes on me, Cris."

Cristine tried—but the hallway sharpened.

A woman stood at the end of it.

Dark hair pulled back. Lab coat wrinkled. Fear etched into her face.

Dr. Halden.

Cristine's knees weakened. "That's her."

Rose whispered, "From the recording."

The woman turned.

For one breathless second, she looked straight at Cristine.

Then the image shattered.

Cristine screamed and dropped to her knees as the field surged. Memories slammed into her—hands holding hers, voices calling her name, alarms, bright lights.

"Make it stop!" she cried.

Skylar knelt beside her. "Listen to my voice."

Cristine shook her head. "They're not mine. They're mine—but not from now."

"That's how memory fields work," Skylar said. "They don't care about time."

Rose pressed her forehead to Cristine's. "You're here. With us."

Cristine focused on Rose's freckles. On the scrape on Nico's knee as he crouched nearby. On Lark's steady breathing.

The images faded.

The field returned to tall grass and soft light.

Cristine lay back, shaking. "She knew me."

Skylar nodded slowly. "She helped create you."

Silence spread across the field.

Nico finally spoke. "I vote we never come back here."

"No," Skylar said. "You will."

Cristine pushed herself upright. "Why?"

"Because this place holds the truth," Skylar said. "And the truth is scattered."

Lark looked at Cristine. "You're not just remembering."

Cristine wiped her eyes. "Then what am I doing?"

Lark's voice was gentle. "You're being remembered."

The grass swayed again.

Far away, something answered.

Skylar stiffened. "They felt that."

Rose stood. "Then let's move."

Skylar nodded. "We've got what we came for."

Cristine glanced back at the field as they walked toward the van.

For a second, she thought she saw a child standing in the grass—barefoot, watching her.

Then the field went still.

CHAPTER 13 — Signal Ghosts

The memory field disappeared behind them like it had never existed.

The Valk rolled back onto the road, tires crunching over loose gravel. Morning light spilled across the hills now, turning fog into thin strands that clung to the trees. Cristine watched them slide past the window, her reflection drifting in and out of the glass.

It blinked late.

She looked away.

No one spoke for several minutes. The van hummed steadily, but beneath it, Cristine felt the deeper vibration again—quiet, patient, waiting.

Rose finally broke the silence. "So... are the ghosts always like that?"

Skylar kept her eyes on the road. "They're not ghosts."

Rose snorted. "They literally showed up, whispered warnings, and vanished."

"Signal ghosts," Skylar corrected. "Fragments left behind when timelines collapse."

Nico leaned forward between the seats. "So pieces of people."

Skylar nodded. "Pieces that still think they're whole."

Cristine hugged her arms. "They were trying to talk to me."

"They will," Skylar said. "More often now."

"That's comforting," Rose muttered.

Skylar slowed near an abandoned rest stop. The concrete building sagged, windows broken, vines crawling up the walls like green veins. A faded map board stood near the entrance, its paint peeling.

"We're stopping," Skylar said.

Nico blinked. "For snacks or existential dread?"

"For shielding," Skylar replied.

They stepped out into the quiet. Wind rustled trash across the cracked pavement. Somewhere inside the building, metal clanged softly, like it was settling.

Skylar opened a storage panel in the van and handed Cristine a small metal band. It looked like a bracelet, thin and dull gray.

"What is it?" Cristine asked.

"Grounding loop," Skylar said. "It helps keep the echoes from pulling you apart."

Cristine slid it onto her wrist. The metal warmed instantly.

The hum inside her softened.

"Oh," she said. "That's... better."

Rose eyed the band. "Can I get one that blocks algebra?"

Skylar smirked. "If only."

They moved into the rest stop building.

Sunlight spilled through broken windows, lighting dust motes that drifted lazily through the air. Old vending machines stood empty and rusted. A map of the state peeled off the wall, curling at the edges.

Cristine stepped carefully.

The air felt thicker here, like walking through invisible water.

Then she heard it.

Her name.

Soft. Close.

She spun around. "Did you hear that?"

Nico shook his head. "Hear what?"

Lark's eyes narrowed. "I did."

The air shimmered near the far wall.

A shape formed—tall, flickering, unfinished. Lines of light traced the outline of a person, breaking apart and reforming.

The signal ghost stepped forward.

It looked like Cristine.

But not quite.

This version was older. Her eyes were tired. Her clothes were torn and scorched, like she'd run through fire.

Rose sucked in a breath. "That's... you."

The ghost raised its head slowly.

"Run," it whispered.

The word echoed, bouncing off the walls even after the mouth stopped moving.

Cristine's chest tightened. "From what?"

The ghost flickered, its image tearing at the edges.

"They're closer than you think," it said. "And you don't always survive."

The building shuddered.

Skylar stepped between them. "That's enough."

The ghost's eyes locked on Cristine's.

"Trust Skylar," it said. "But don't trust the ending."

Then it shattered into static.

The air snapped back to normal.

Cristine staggered.

Rose grabbed her. "Okay. I officially hate meeting future-you."

Skylar's jaw was tight. "That wasn't a random echo."

Cristine swallowed. "It knew things."

"Yes," Skylar said. "Which means C.O.D. is pushing timelines harder."

Nico frowned. "Because of her?"

Skylar nodded. "Because she's changing outcomes."

Cristine looked down at the bracelet, faintly glowing on her wrist. "I don't want to change anything."

Skylar met her eyes. "You already have."

A low buzz rolled across the rest stop.

Skylar stiffened. "Drones."

They ran.

Back in the van, Skylar hit the ignition as lights flared outside the broken windows.

The Valk surged forward just as two drones rose over the roof, their beams sweeping the lot.

Cristine glanced back through the rear window.

For a second, dozens of signal ghosts stood in the doorway of the rest stop—watching her leave.

Some looked relieved.

Others looked afraid.

The van sped away, leaving the building—and the ghosts—behind.

Cristine pressed her hand to the glass.

"They're not done with me," she whispered.

Skylar's voice was steady. "No. They're just getting started."

CHAPTER 14 — The Split

The road ahead shimmered.

At first, Cristine thought it was heat rising off the pavement. Then the shimmer bent to the side, like someone dragging a finger through wet paint.

Skylar slowed the Valk. "Everyone, stay still."

The van rolled forward inch by inch. The hum beneath the floor deepened, vibrating through Cristine's shoes and into her legs.

"What is that?" Rose asked, leaning toward the windshield.

"The split," Skylar said. "Where outcomes stop agreeing."

Nico squinted. "You make it sound like the road's arguing with itself."

Skylar didn't smile.

Ahead of them, the asphalt cracked—not open, but wrong. Two versions of the same road overlapped, slightly out of sync. On one, the center line was faded yellow. On the other, it was bright and new. The trees along the shoulder doubled, leaves fluttering in different directions.

Cristine's head throbbed.

She saw it clearly now—two paths, both real.

Both pulling at her.

"I don't like this," Rose said quietly.

"No one does," Skylar replied. "That's why we don't stop here."

She turned the wheel.

The Valk crossed the invisible line.

The world lurched.

Cristine gasped as gravity twisted sideways. Her stomach dropped, like she'd missed a step on stairs that weren't there. The hum spiked, sharp and loud, rattling her teeth.

Outside, the trees blurred.

Then split.

One set rushed past on the left. Another slid backward on the right.

"Skylar!" Nico shouted. "We're in two places!"

"Not yet," Skylar said, gripping the wheel. "But we're close."

Cristine squeezed her eyes shut.

Images slammed into her—two versions of the van, two sets of headlights, two Skylar voices shouting different commands.

"Hold on!"

"No—brake!"

Cristine screamed.

The bracelet on her wrist burned hot.

She opened her eyes.

The van flickered, edges tearing like paper. Rose's hand blurred in and out of focus. Nico's face doubled, then snapped back.

Lark grabbed the back of Cristine's seat. "She's splitting."

Skylar shouted, "Cris—look at me!"

Cristine forced her gaze forward.

Skylar's eyes were steady in the mirror. Real. Anchored.

"Choose," Skylar said.

Cristine shook her head. "I can't see which one's right!"

"None of them are," Skylar said. "That's the point."

The road ahead forked—not left and right, but *overlapping*. One path dipped into shadow. The other glowed faintly blue.

Cristine felt herself being pulled apart—one version of her leaning toward each road.

Rose grabbed her arm. "Stay here. With us."

Nico shouted, "Pick the one without the creepy glow!"

Cristine laughed once, sharp and panicked. "That's not helping!"

The hum roared.

The world slowed.

Raindrops hung in the air like glass beads. The trees froze mid-sway. Even Skylar's breath paused.

Cristine stood inside the moment.

Two futures pressed against her chest.

In one, the van swerved too late.

In the other—

She didn't know.

"I don't want either," Cristine whispered.

The bracelet flared bright.

Lark's voice cut through the stillness. "Then make a third."

Cristine inhaled.

She focused on the van—the feel of the seat, Rose's grip on her arm, the sound of Nico breathing too fast. She pushed everything else away.

Not left.

Not right.

Now.

The hum snapped.

Time crashed forward.

The Valk surged straight ahead, the overlapping roads tearing apart behind them like fabric ripping down the middle.

Cristine collapsed back into her seat, gasping.

The world steadied.

Trees lined the road again—single, solid, real.

Skylar let out a shaky breath. "You did it."

Rose stared at Cristine. "You just told reality 'no.'"

Nico blinked. "I didn't know that was an option."

Cristine wiped her eyes. "I didn't either."

Behind them, the split sealed shut, the shimmer fading like it had never been there.

But Cristine could still feel it.

Not gone.

Just waiting for the next choice.

CHAPTER 15 — Echo Protocol

They didn't stop the van right away.

Skylar drove until the road narrowed into a ribbon of cracked asphalt cutting through dense forest. Tall pines leaned inward, their branches tangling overhead and blocking most of the light. The sun hung low, turning the air gold and dusty.

When she finally pulled over, the Valk idled beside a dry creek bed filled with smooth gray stones.

"Out," Skylar said. "But stay close."

Cristine stepped down carefully. The ground felt solid—normal—but the hum still lingered beneath it, faint and steady.

Rose stretched her arms. "I vote for places that don't try to rip us in half."

Skylar ignored her and knelt by the creek. She placed a small device on a flat rock. It unfolded with a soft click, thin metal arms spreading outward like spider legs.

"What's that?" Nico asked.

"Echo protocol," Skylar said. "If you're going to keep surviving splits, we need rules."

Cristine's stomach tightened. "Rules sound good."

Skylar activated the device.

The air shimmered above the creek. The stones reflected twice—once where they were, once where they *almost* were.

"Rule one," Skylar said, pointing to the shimmer. "Echoes follow attention. What you focus on gets louder."

Cristine nodded slowly. "That's why they rush in when I panic."

"Exactly," Skylar said. "Fear is a beacon."

Rose frowned. "That's... not comforting."

Skylar continued. "Rule two: echoes can't cross stable anchors."

She tossed a coin into the creek.

It splashed.

The shimmer rippled—but didn't follow.

"Water grounds them," Skylar explained. "So do people. Physical contact matters."

Rose immediately grabbed Cristine's hand. "Noted."

Cristine squeezed back.

Skylar stood and faced Cristine. "Rule three is the hardest."

She stepped back, creating space between them.

"Never answer an echo directly."

Cristine stiffened. "Even if it's me?"

"Especially if it's you," Skylar said.

As if on cue, the air behind Cristine shifted.

A faint outline appeared—thin, flickering, unfinished.

Another Cristine stood there.

Her clothes were darker. Her eyes looked older. Tired.

Rose sucked in a breath. "She's back."

The echo tilted its head.

"You survived the split," it said. "That wasn't supposed to happen."

Cristine's chest tightened. "What happens if I answer?"

Skylar's voice was sharp. "You trade places."

The echo smiled sadly. "Just for a moment."

Cristine's hands shook.

"I don't want your moment," she said.

The echo stepped closer. The air grew cold.

"Then you'll lose someone else," it whispered.

Nico moved in front of Cristine without thinking. "Nope. Hard no."

The echo flickered.

Skylar slammed her palm onto the device.

The shimmer collapsed.

The echo shattered into static and vanished.

Cristine sagged forward, breath shaky.

Rose wrapped her in a hug. "You did good."

Cristine whispered, "It knew things."

Skylar nodded. "They all do."

Skylar shut down the device and looked at Cristine seriously.

"Echo protocol exists for one reason," she said. "To keep you from becoming one of them."

Cristine swallowed. "Is that what happens if I mess up?"

"Yes," Skylar said. "You don't die. You fracture."

Nico grimaced. "That might be worse."

Skylar glanced at the trees. Shadows stretched long between them, too still.

"We're out of time here," she said. "C.O.D. won't wait."

Cristine looked at the creek, at the stones, at her reflection moving when it was supposed to.

"I don't want to disappear," she said quietly.

Skylar met her eyes. "Then we make sure you don't."

The hum shifted again—restless now.

From somewhere deep in the woods, a branch snapped.

Rose tightened her grip on Cristine's hand. "Tell me we're leaving."

Skylar already had the keys in her hand.

"We are," she said. "But next time, you don't just react."

Cristine nodded, heart pounding. "Next time, I choose."

They climbed back into the Valk as shadows stretched across the road.

Behind them, the creek shimmered once.

Then went still.

CHAPTER 16 — The Split Signal

They felt it before they saw it.

The hum changed pitch—higher, sharper—like a note pulled too tight. The Valk's dashboard lights flickered, then steadied. Skylar's hands tightened on the wheel.

"Signal's splitting," she said.

Rose leaned forward. "That sounds bad."

"It is," Skylar replied. "Two broadcasts. Same source."

Cristine's chest tightened. The bracelet on her wrist warmed, then cooled, pulsing in uneven beats.

"I feel it," Cristine said. "It's like... being called twice."

Nico frowned. "By who?"

Cristine shook her head. "By me."

The road climbed into rocky hills. Pines thinned, giving way to scrub and exposed stone. Ahead, a tall radio tower rose from the ridge, its red lights blinking through drifting mist.

The blink wasn't steady.

It doubled.

One light flashed early. The other lagged behind.

Skylar slowed. "That tower shouldn't be active."

Lark's eyes tracked the lights. "It's not. Not all the way."

They parked behind a line of boulders. Wind whistled through cracks in the rock, carrying the smell of dust and ozone.

Skylar cut the engine. "We don't approach yet."

Cristine stepped out anyway, drawn toward the ridge. The air tugged at her, pulling left and right at the same time.

The tower shimmered.

For a moment, there were two towers—slightly offset, overlapping like reflections in bad glass.

"Whoa," Nico muttered. "That's new."

"No," Skylar said. "That's the signal tearing."

Cristine staggered as pressure built behind her eyes.

Two voices whispered her name.

Not echoes.

Commands.

Rose grabbed her arm. "Cris—stay with us."

Cristine nodded, forcing her gaze down to the dirt beneath her shoes. Pebbles vibrated, rolling a few inches, then stopping.

"Skylar," Cristine said, breath shaking. "One of them is louder."

Skylar moved beside her. "Which one?"

Cristine pointed. "The one that doesn't care if we're here."

Skylar cursed quietly. "C.O.D. injected a control signal."

Nico's eyes widened. "So it's fighting itself."

"Yes," Skylar said. "And you're in the middle."

The wind died.

Silence pressed in so hard Cristine's ears rang.

The tower's lights froze mid-blink.

Time slowed.

Cristine saw two paths unfold in front of her—not roads this time, but *signals*. One glowed cold blue, steady and clean. The other flickered white, unstable but alive.

The blue one pulled harder.

Safer.

Empty.

Skylar's voice cut through the stillness. "Don't follow the clean one."

Cristine swallowed. "Why?"

"Because that's erasure," Skylar said. "No echoes. No pain. No you."

The white signal flared.

It hurt to look at—but it felt real.

Cristine clenched her fists. "I don't want to disappear."

"Then listen," Skylar said. "Not answer. Listen."

Cristine took a shaky breath and let the sounds wash over her without reaching back. The whispers rose, then faded, like waves breaking and retreating.

The white signal steadied.

The blue one cracked.

The tower shuddered.

Lights burst back into motion.

Time snapped forward.

Cristine collapsed to one knee, gasping.

Rose knelt beside her. "You okay?"

Cristine nodded weakly. "I didn't choose either."

Skylar smiled, fierce and proud. "Good."

The tower went dark.

Then, far off in the valley, another light blinked on.

Then another.

Lark's voice was calm but tight. "They're copying the signal."

Skylar stood, eyes scanning the horizon. "That means they're learning."

Nico groaned. "Great. The bad guys are adapting."

Cristine stared at the distant lights, her bracelet pulsing faster.

"I can still feel it," she said. "Like it's unfinished."

Skylar met her gaze. "It is. And now they know you can interfere."

Cristine's stomach sank. "So what happens next?"

Skylar opened the van door. "Next, they stop trying to contain you."

The hum deepened—stronger than before.

From the ridge, a low mechanical whine drifted upward.

Drones.

Rose squeezed Cristine's hand. "Tell me we're running."

Skylar started the engine. "Already are."

As the Valk tore down the trail, Cristine looked back at the tower.

For a split second, she saw another version of herself standing beneath it—watching her go.

Then the image shattered.

And the signal followed them into the dark.

CHAPTER 17 — Static Between

The Valk didn't slow down until the road disappeared into dirt again.

Skylar cut the headlights and steered by memory alone. Trees rushed past, their trunks flashing pale in the moonlight. Branches scraped the sides of the van like reaching hands.

Cristine sat rigid, the hum inside her no longer steady.

It wavered.

Like a radio between stations.

Rose leaned close. "You're shaking."

Cristine nodded. "It's not one signal anymore. It's… space between them."

Skylar glanced at her in the mirror. "That's worse."

"Great," Nico muttered. "We've upgraded from bad to worse."

Skylar slammed the brakes.

The van skidded to a stop beside a narrow ravine. A broken guardrail hung over the edge, twisted like it had been bent by something strong—and careless.

Mist rose from below, swallowing the sound of rushing water.

Skylar killed the engine. "Everyone out. Quiet."

They stepped into cold air. The ravine dropped away only a few feet from the road, a black gap that seemed deeper than it should be.

Cristine edged closer and peered down.

For a second, she saw stars.

Not reflections.

Actual stars, as the sky had opened beneath her feet.

She staggered back. "The ground isn't right."

"That's static between," Skylar said. "Where timelines brush past each other without touching."

Rose hugged herself. "I don't like places that pretend to be other places."

Skylar crouched and tossed a rock into the ravine.

It fell.

Then slowed.

Then vanished without a sound.

Nico stared. "Did it fall forever?"

"No," Skylar said. "It fell nowhere."

The hum inside Cristine surged.

Whispers filled her ears—not words, just feeling. Regret. Fear. Relief.

All at once.

She pressed her hands to her head. "They're not echoes. They're... leftovers."

Skylar's voice was sharp. "Focus. On me."

Cristine forced her gaze up.

Skylar stood solid against the dark, boots planted, shoulders squared.

The noise softened.

Rose let out a breath. "Okay. That helps."

Lark spoke quietly. "But it's spreading."

Mist crept up the ravine, curling over the road. The air thickened, bending light into faint ripples.

Shapes moved inside it.

Not ghosts.

Gaps.

Like pieces missing from the world.

Nico backed up. "Those are definitely not friendly."

Skylar snapped open a case and pulled out two small metal stakes. She slammed them into the dirt on either side of the road.

They hummed, throwing off a dull orange glow.

"What are those?" Rose asked.

"Anchors," Skylar said. "Temporary."

The mist recoiled—but didn't disappear.

Cristine's bracelet burned hot.

"I can feel something pulling," she said. "Like it wants me in the middle."

Skylar nodded grimly. "That's because you're the bridge."

Cristine swallowed. "Between what?"

"Between what survived," Skylar said, "and what didn't."

The mist surged forward.

Cristine cried out as the ground beneath her feet flickered—solid, then hollow, then solid again.

Rose grabbed her jacket. "Stay here. Don't step!"

Cristine froze, heart hammering.

Below her, the road thinned to nothing, revealing darkness shot through with distant lights.

Other worlds.

Other endings.

Skylar moved fast. "Cris—jump back. Now."

Cristine hesitated.

The pull intensified.

For a terrifying second, she felt herself slipping—like gravity had changed its mind.

Then Nico shouted, "I've got you!"

He grabbed her arm. Rose grabbed her other side.

They pulled together.

Cristine stumbled back onto solid ground as the road snapped whole again.

The mist shrieked—not a sound, but a pressure that made her ears ring.

Skylar yanked the anchors free. "In the van. Now!"

They ran.

The Valk roared to life as the mist swallowed the road behind them.

Cristine looked back through the rear window.

The ravine was gone.

In its place was a normal stretch of forest road.

Too normal.

Cristine shivered. "It's pretending again."

Skylar nodded. "It always does."

Rose leaned her head against Cristine's shoulder. "Next time, let's go somewhere boring."

Cristine tried to smile.

The hum inside her settled—but it didn't disappear.

It waited.

Between signals.

Between worlds.

CHAPTER 18 — The Hollow Dream

At first, it felt like falling.

But slower.

Like the air had turned into water, thick and heavy, and the world below her didn't care whether she landed—or disappeared.

Cristine opened her eyes.

The tunnel was gone.

She stood in the middle of a gymnasium.

The same one from before—but perfect this time.

The floor gleamed like glass. The banners hung smooth and bright, without a single wrinkle. The lights above burned steadily and warm.

The scoreboard glowed red.

00:00:01

00:00:02

Counting forward again.

Cristine exhaled, her breath echoing softly in the open space.

Her reflection stared back at her from the polished floor.

Only—

It blinked first.

Cristine flinched.

Then she realized she wasn't alone.

Someone sat at the scorer's table, tapping a pencil against a clipboard. The sound echoed, sharp and steady.

Tap.

Tap.

Tap.

Skylar.

Or something shaped like her.

"Am I dreaming?" Cristine asked.

Skylar looked up.

Her eyes weren't right. They glowed faintly, like light seen through fog or water.

"You're remembering," she said.

Cristine frowned. "I don't remember this."

"You don't yet."

The scoreboard flickered.

The numbers rewound.

00:00:02

00:00:01

00:00:00

Cristine's breath caught. "Where are the others?"

Skylar—no, the echo of her—smiled faintly.

"Ahead of you," she said. "Behind you. Every version has its own distance."

Cristine's stomach twisted. "You're not her."

"I'm what she left behind," the echo said calmly. "We all are."

The lights overhead buzzed softly. Dust drifted through the beams like tiny falling stars.

Cristine turned slowly, scanning the gym.

Each doorway along the walls pulsed faintly blue.

A dozen exits.

A dozen paths.

Leading nowhere.

She walked to the nearest doorway.

A classroom appeared beyond it. Empty desks. Chairs pushed in neatly, like class had just ended.

She stepped back and tried another.

A hallway stretched beyond the door, curving in on itself like a spiral drawn by a shaking hand.

Cristine turned around.

The gym was gone.

She stood in The Hollow.

The same bunker.

But alive.

Screens covered the walls, flickering with moving faces.

Her face.

Dozens of them.

Each one whispered something too soft to understand.

"Stop," Cristine whispered.

The whispers grew louder.

Not words.

Versions.

A dozen Cristines stared back at her from the monitors.

One looked older.

One was crying.

One smiled faintly, blood drying at her temple.

One pressed her hand to the glass, her breath fogging the screen as she mouthed something soundless.

Cristine stumbled backward, her heart racing. "No. This isn't—"

"It is," a voice said behind her.

She turned.

Another Cristine stood in the doorway, haloed by static light.

The echo.

"You called me," the echo said softly. "You keep calling me."

"I didn't mean to."

"Meaning doesn't change consequence," the echo replied. "You opened the bridge when you chose to remember."

Cristine's throat ached. "What are you?"

The echo smiled—a perfect, empty imitation of comfort.

"The version of you that stayed."

The lights in the bunker began to pulse.

Blue.

White.

Black.

With each flicker, the echo stepped closer. Her face blurred, shifting between kindness and absence. Her voice warped slightly, like a damaged recording.

Cristine backed into the wall. "Stay away."

The echo stopped just out of reach.

"You can't outrun yourself, Cristine."

Then, almost gently:

"Not yet."

The floor vanished.

Cristine was underwater—or something like it.

Everything moved slowly. Weightless. Silent.

Her hair floated around her face, catching light that shouldn't exist here.

Beneath her, shapes drifted.

People-shaped.

Familiar.

The squad.

Rose looked up through the shimmer, her goggles reflecting blue light.

Nico hovered nearby, his coin spinning like a tiny sun trapped in slow motion.

Lark reached toward Cristine, her fingers almost—but not quite—touching.

Skylar watched from a distance, calculating, unreadable.

And then—

The others.

The echoes.

Two of everything.

Two sets of faces.

Two sets of eyes.

Two sets of choices.

Cristine screamed, but bubbles spilled from her mouth instead of sound.

The echoes swam closer, their hands reaching out.

For one heartbeat, she saw herself clearly.

The original.

The copy.

Both blurred into one.

Then—

A hand grabbed hers.

Real.

Solid.

"Cris!" Rose's voice cut through the water. "Wake up!"

Cristine jolted upright with a gasp.

Air tore back into her lungs like fire.

The cold tunnel floor burned against her palms.

Darkness.

The tunnel.

Rose's hands were on her shoulders, her eyes wide. "You were twitching. You said something about not being real."

Cristine dragged in a shaky breath. "It felt real."

Skylar stood at the far end of the tunnel, her face tense. "Dream or not, Chronyx uses memory like a signal. If it found a way in—"

"It wasn't just memory," Cristine interrupted, her voice shaking. "It was me. She said she was what I left behind."

Nico muttered, "So... you're haunted by your own software update. Awesome."

Rose shot him a look, but even she didn't have a comeback ready.

Lark's voice was calm, almost reverent. "Dreams are safe places for things that can't exist yet. Maybe she's not your enemy."

Cristine shook her head. "She's not my friend either."

Silence filled the tunnel again.

Heavy—but human.

Skylar stepped closer, her voice low. "Next time you see her—don't run. Learn what she wants."

Cristine met her eyes. "And if what she wants is me?"

Skylar hesitated, then said, "Then we'll make sure she never gets that far."

Somewhere deep in the tunnel, metal groaned—long and slow—like the world exhaling.

Nico muttered, "Cool. That's not ominous at all."

But even he didn't laugh this time.

Far beneath the concrete, a low pulse answered.

Steady.

Waiting.

Cristine closed her eyes, trying not to match its rhythm.

For a while, she almost convinced herself it was only her heartbeat—

Until she realized she could still hear it after she fell asleep.

CHAPTER 19 — Gray Morning

Cristine didn't wake all at once.

The darkness thinned slowly, like fog lifting off cold ground. Sound returned in pieces—water dripping somewhere, the low hum of machinery, the soft scrape of boots on concrete.

She opened her eyes.

The tunnel ceiling arched overhead, cracked and stained. Dim work lights lined the walls, their glow uneven and tired. The air smelled damp and metallic, like rust after rain.

She was lying on her back.

Rose sat cross-legged beside her, chewing on a sleeve. When she noticed Cristine's eyes open, her face broke into relief.

"Oh good," Rose said. "You're back in the correct universe."

Cristine swallowed. "How long was I out?"

"Long enough for Nico to narrate your twitching like a sports event," Rose said.

"High drama," Nico added from a few feet away. "Very suspenseful."

Cristine tried to sit up.

Skylar was there instantly, steadying her shoulder. "Easy."

Cristine winced. "My head feels... stretched."

Skylar nodded. "You crossed too deep."

Lark knelt nearby, watching Cristine closely. "You weren't alone."

Cristine exhaled slowly. "No. I know."

They helped her sit against the tunnel wall. Cold seeped through her jacket, grounding her. She pressed her palms to the concrete, focusing on the rough texture.

"What did you see?" Rose asked.

Cristine hesitated.

The images were already fading at the edges, like dreams do—but some pieces stuck sharp and bright.

"A gym," she said. "Perfect. Like nothing bad ever happened there."

Skylar's expression tightened. "That's a constructed memory space."

"There was a version of you," Cristine continued. "But not... you. An echo."

Nico raised his eyebrows. "Did it try to kill you?"

"No," Cristine said quietly. "It tried to *explain* me."

Skylar stiffened. "What did it say?"

Cristine looked down at her hands. "That it's what was left behind."

Silence followed.

Lark spoke softly. "Then it exists because you moved forward."

Cristine nodded. "That's what it felt like."

Skylar exhaled through her nose. "Chronyx didn't just experiment on time. They experimented on *outcomes*."

Rose frowned. "So... different versions of Cris were tested?"

Skylar met her eyes. "Some were kept. Some weren't."

Cristine's stomach turned.

"Why show me now?" Cristine asked. "Why not before?"

Skylar's voice was quiet. "Because you're strong enough to survive it now."

A distant clang echoed through the tunnel.

Metal on metal.

Skylar's head snapped up. "We're not alone."

Nico stood, peering into the darkness. "Please tell me that was a rat."

Another sound answered.

Slower.

Heavier.

Lark's eyes unfocused for a moment. "Movement. Down the west passage."

Skylar grabbed her pack. "We move. Now."

Cristine pushed herself to her feet, legs unsteady but solid. The hum inside her was back—but different.

Not pulling.

Waiting.

They hurried down the tunnel, boots splashing through shallow puddles. Water dripped from overhead pipes, each drop echoing too loudly in the narrow space.

Cristine glanced back.

For just a second, she thought she saw someone standing where she'd been lying.

Another her.

Watching.

Then the light shifted, and the space was empty.

They emerged into a wider chamber where old machinery sat silent and half-buried in dust. Rusted panels lined the walls, their labels worn smooth.

Skylar slowed. "This is a wake zone."

Nico frowned. "That sounds like a funeral thing."

"It's where echoes gather before stabilizing," Skylar said. "Or collapsing."

Cristine felt the air thicken again.

The hum rose slightly, spreading through the room like a breath being held.

Rose moved closer to Cristine. "You okay?"

Cristine nodded. "I think so."

But she wasn't sure.

Because beneath the hum, beneath the quiet—

She could feel it.

The one that stayed.

Still listening.

CHAPTER 20 — Fault Lines

The ridge trail twisted upward in broken switchbacks, the kind that made it feel like you were walking everywhere except where you needed to go. Mist hugged the ground, thick and cold, sliding between the trees in silver curls.

Skylar led the way.

Her steps were silent, even on loose gravel. A rifle rested across her shoulder, and her free hand stayed close to her jacket pocket—where the detonator waited.

Always ready.

Always tense.

Rose followed behind her, grumbling under her breath. "Whoever invented hills clearly hated people."

Nico walked backward for a stretch, waving his arms like a nature show host. "And here we see the rare band of preteens, guided by a grumpy ex–mad scientist, migrating toward certain doom in their natural habitat— fog and regret."

"Face forward before you die dramatically," Rose said, giving him a shove.

Lark moved quietly a few steps behind them, her eyes never stopping. She scanned every tree, every shadow, even though she hadn't slept.

Cristine walked last.

Her backpack straps dug into her shoulders, but she barely noticed. Her thoughts wouldn't slow down. Every time she blinked, she saw the echo again.

Her own face.

Smiling.

Waiting.

Halfway up the ridge, Skylar raised a hand.

They stopped.

"Break here," Skylar said softly. "We'll scout from the overlook before heading to the substation."

Rose dropped her bag and sat hard on a mossy rock. "Finally. My lungs were starting to unionize."

Nico collapsed beside her. "Mine quit two turns ago. I'm powered entirely by sarcasm now."

Skylar gave them a look sharp enough to cut stone. "Stay near the path."

Then she turned to Cristine. "You're with me."

Cristine blinked. "Why?"

"Because you ask fewer questions when you're nervous," Skylar said, already moving into the trees.

Rose grinned. "Oof. Mentorship or emotional damage?"

Lark answered quietly, "Both."

In the Trees

The woods swallowed sound.

Fog thickened until the trail faded into little more than a pale suggestion under their boots. Branches creaked overhead, bending slightly in the wind, as if listening.

Skylar moved with careful precision, scanning the ground, the treeline, the spaces between.

Cristine tried to keep pace. Her fingertips shimmered faintly, the glow dim but stubborn.

"Was it always this quiet?" Cristine asked.

Skylar didn't turn around. "No. That's what worries me."

They stepped into a small clearing, round and tight, ringed by tall pines.

At its center lay the wreckage of a collapsed communications mast. Twisted metal jutted from the ground, blackened and scorched.

Skylar crouched and brushed ash from a small metal plate.

A faded logo caught the thin light.

CYREX INDUSTRIES.

Cristine knelt beside her. "You knew this was here."

Skylar's jaw tightened. "I built it."

Cristine froze. "You—what?"

Skylar stood slowly. "Before Chronyx. Before everything went wrong."

Cristine stared at the wreckage differently now.

"This was a relay," Skylar continued. "A test node. We used it to map signal bleed between systems."

Cristine swallowed. "And it failed."

Skylar nodded once. "Catastrophically."

The hum beneath Cristine's skin shifted, reacting to the broken tower like it recognized an old scar.

Rose's voice drifted from the trail. "Uh, hate to interrupt the emotional reveal, but something feels... off."

Skylar straightened. "Because it is."

The ground vibrated faintly.

Not shaking.

Listening.

Cristine closed her eyes for half a second—and felt it.

Lines beneath the soil.

Invisible cracks stretching outward, overlapping, pulling.

Fault lines.

"Skylar," she whispered. "This place isn't dead."

Skylar met her gaze, grim. "No. It's waking up."

Somewhere deeper in the forest, metal groaned.

Slow.

Heavy.

Nico called out, trying to sound casual. "Sooo... is this the part where we leave?"

Skylar reached for her detonator.

Cristine felt the hum rise again, sharper now, tugging at her thoughts.

And beneath it all—

A familiar presence.

Patient.

Waiting.

CHAPTER 21 — Nightfall

By the time they reached the upper ridge, daylight had thinned to ash. The forest looked half-drowned in fog, the kind that swallowed sound and left only breath. Every tree was a silhouette, every shadow uncertain.

The group stopped beneath a slanted pine, its branches black against a bruised sky. The temperature had dropped sharply enough that even Rose stopped complaining. Their breath came out in faint ghosts.

"Okay," Nico said, voice low. "Quick survey—does anyone else feel like we're stuck in a cut episode of *Stranger Things*?"

Rose gave a weak laugh. "If we start hearing whispering, I'm throwing you first."

"You say that like it's a threat," Nico said. "I'd make an excellent human distraction."

Skylar crouched near a rock ledge, scanning the slope below through a small handheld monitor. The screen bled static, but faint red traces pulsed along the lower valley.

"Heat signatures?" Lark asked.

Skylar nodded once. "Residual. Cyrex drones sweep here every two hours. We've got one before they loop back."

Cristine stood beside her, peering into the fog. "What's that sound?"

At first, no one heard it. Then it came—soft, low, rhythmic. Not mechanical. Not wind.

A pulse.

Rose frowned. "Please tell me that's thunder."

"It's not," Lark whispered.

The hum wove through the fog, vibrating faintly in their ribs.

Cristine recognized it instantly.

Chronyx.

Her skin prickled with static, a faint blue shimmer returning to her fingertips like old blood remembering how to pulse.

Skylar saw it. "Stay calm. It's feedback from the field."

Cristine shook her head. "No. It's listening again."

Nico swallowed hard. "How do you know?"

"Because it's saying my name."

And then they heard it—soft, distorted, like a recording echoing from far away.

Cristine.

It wasn't loud. It didn't need to be.

It came from the fog itself.

Rose spun, flashlight cutting across the trees. "Nope. Nope, we are not doing this tonight."

The beam caught nothing. Just mist, silver, and empty.

"Stay together," Skylar ordered, her tone sharp. "Don't respond to it."

Cristine's pulse was in her ears. "It sounds like me."

Nico's humor cracked at the edges. "Cool. You're haunting yourself. Love that journey for you."

The fog thickened, pressing close like breath on glass. Shapes moved within it—slow, wrong, like memories trying to stand upright.

One of them shifted toward Lark's side.

"Skylar," Lark said softly, "something's walking with us."

The shape tilted its head.

Her head.

It was Lark—same braid, same expression—only too still.

Lark's breath hitched. "That's not me."

Skylar raised her weapon. "Eyes down. No sudden—"

The duplicate flickered, static crawling across its outline. It smiled faintly, then spoke in a perfect copy of Lark's voice:

"You left us behind."

Lark froze.

Cristine stepped forward, instinct more than reason. "Don't look at it too long," she whispered. "It's just—"

Her words died.

Another shape stepped through the fog.

Rose's face. Then Nico's. Then Skylar's. Then—hers.

Five silhouettes. All moving in sync.

Each one just slightly out of rhythm.

The hum deepened until it felt like the air might crack.

"Skylar," Rose hissed, "what do we do?"

"Keep walking," Skylar said through gritted teeth. "They're echoes. They only react if you—"

"—notice them," her echo finished, perfectly overlapping her voice.

The real Skylar flinched.

Cristine's stomach turned to ice. The shimmer at her fingertips spread up her arms now, veins lit in faint blue like circuitry.

"Cris—" Lark reached for her. "You're phasing."

Cristine looked down—her outline blurred, pulsing in and out of sync.

She felt light, as if gravity were a suggestion.

The echo version of her stepped closer, raising a trembling hand.

"Stop," Cristine whispered. "Don't—"

Her double touched her shoulder.

It was like touching ice and lightning at once.

A flash of memory—voices, faces, a lab full of white light—then gone.

Cristine stumbled backward, gasping. "She—she showed me something."

Skylar moved fast, grabbing her wrist and pulling her back. "Don't engage! That's how they map new data!"

Rose grabbed Nico's arm. "Define 'new data.'"

"Us," Skylar snapped. "Every reaction, every fear— it's all code they can copy."

Nico's voice was tight now, no jokes left. "Then we stop giving them anything to work with."

Skylar turned sharply toward the ridge. "Move! We need elevation before the field stabilizes—go!"

They ran.

The echoes followed—gliding rather than running, faces flickering in and out like faulty projections.

Each footstep sounded a heartbeat late.

Cristine's lungs burned. The hum was inside her now, pressing behind her eyes, whispering in static.

She could still hear her name—over and over, softer each time.

By the time they reached the upper ridge, the air thinned. The fog broke in patches.

When Cristine dared to look back, the echoes had stopped at the treeline, watching.

They didn't vanish.

They just waited.

They collapsed near a ridge of black stone. The night sky stretched above, scattered with faint, static stars.

Nico dropped his bag and sat hard. "Okay. I'm officially out of brave."

Rose didn't answer. Her hands shook as she reloaded her flashlight battery for the tenth time.

Lark was staring into the dark, lips moving soundlessly.

Cristine sat down beside her. "Lark?"

Lark blinked slowly. "They weren't angry."

Cristine frowned. "What?"

"The echoes," Lark whispered. "They weren't chasing. They were mirroring. Like... trying to remember us."

Skylar exhaled, leaning against a tree. "That's exactly what they're doing."

Cristine rubbed her arms as the faint glow faded slowly. "What happens when they remember everything?"

Skylar looked out into the fog where their doubles still waited.

"Then we stop existing twice," she said quietly. "And only one version walks away."

Silence.

Only the sound of wind over leaves—and something deeper beneath it, like a heartbeat still counting down.

CHAPTER 22 — Between Versions

Cristine dreamed—but not deeply.

The world felt thin, like paper rubbed too smooth.

She stood in a wide open space, neither dark nor bright. The ground beneath her feet reflected light like calm water, though it felt solid.

She wasn't alone.

Someone stood across from her.

Not an echo this time.

Not exactly.

The girl looked like Cristine—but younger. Her hair was shorter. Her eyes sharper. She stood with her hands clenched, ready to run or fight.

"Are you real?" Cristine asked.

The girl shrugged. "Depends which version you ask."

Cristine's chest tightened. "You're... me."

"Close enough," the girl said. "I'm between."

The air shimmered softly.

Cristine glanced around. "Between what?"

"Outcomes," the girl replied. "Choices. You keep bending them."

Cristine shook her head. "I'm just trying to survive."

The girl's expression softened. "So was I."

They stood in silence, reflections rippling beneath their feet.

"Why do you keep showing up?" Cristine asked.

"Because you're changing the rules," the other Cristine said. "And that affects all of us."

Cristine swallowed. "What happens if I stop?"

The girl looked away. "Then everything settles."

"That sounds good," Cristine said.

The girl met her gaze again. "It's not."

The space flickered.

Cristine felt the pull again—gentle, dangerous.

"I don't want to lose anyone," Cristine whispered.

The other version nodded. "Then don't choose alone."

The world folded inward.

Cristine woke with a sharp breath.

Gray light filled the shelter. Morning mist curled through the broken doorway.

Rose sat nearby, rubbing sleep from her eyes. "You were talking again."

Cristine pushed herself up. "What did I say?"

"Something about not choosing alone," Rose said. "Which is either deep or worrying."

Skylar stood at the doorway, watching the fog lift. "We're moving."

Cristine joined her, staring out at the valley.

The hum inside her had settled—but it felt wider now, like it reached farther than before.

Between versions.

Between choices.

And for the first time, Cristine understood something clearly:

She wasn't the only one affected by what she did.

She was connected to all of them.

CHAPTER 23 — Greaves' Directive

The command floor pulsed like a heartbeat.

Not a human one.

Lights flickered in perfect rhythm with the monitors lining the walls, washing the room in pale white and cold blue. The air hummed with power, sharp and metallic.

Agent Greaves stood at the center of it all.

Still. Precise. Every inch of him looked planned.

"Run it again," he said quietly.

An analyst swallowed, then tapped her console. A holographic map burst into the air—mountain ridges glowing blue, heat signatures marked in red.

Five small blips moved steadily east.

"They're still fragmented," she said. "Using old Cyrex hardware. Handheld dampeners. Clever, but temporary."

Greaves studied the map. "And the driver?"

"Unidentified. Facial recognition failed three cross-matches. Military-grade interference."

Greaves's fingers tapped the console once.

"That's not interference," he said calmly. "That's design."

He stepped closer. Light fractured across his face, sharp and clean, like glass cut with purpose.

"Pull every archived personnel file tied to Project Chronyx," he said. "Caretaker profiles first."

The analyst hesitated. "Sir... those files are sealed."

Greaves didn't raise his voice. "So unseal them."

The hum of the room deepened as restricted systems unlocked. Rows of names flickered by—corrupted photos, broken data.

Then one file stabilized.

SKYLAR M. ROWE — CARETAKER UNIT 9B STATUS: TERMINATED

Greaves smiled faintly.

"There you are."

He stared at the image—Skylar, younger, unscarred, eyes bright with belief.

"Sir," the analyst said carefully, "records confirm a fatal detonation at Site Theta."

Greaves didn't look away. "No. She made them think she died. That's what I trained her to do."

He turned toward the observation window.

Beyond the glass, twelve containment pods glowed faint blue. Inside them, human-shaped forms flickered in and out of focus.

Not bodies.

Echoes.

A junior tech spoke from the far console. "Sir, the prototypes are destabilizing. We can't maintain coherence past ninety seconds."

"Extend the loop," Greaves said.

"Sir, the energy cost—"

"Is irrelevant."

He watched the pods closely. "Every second they exist, they remember more. And memory is our most valuable weapon."

The analyst shifted nervously. "If we continue pulling echo signatures, we risk a bleed event. Time displacement—"

Greaves turned. "Do you know why Chronyx failed the first time?"

No one answered.

"They tried to contain time," he continued, pacing slowly. "They treated it like a straight line. Measurable. Obedient."

He stopped beside the glass.

"But time adapts."

His hand rested on the pod surface. Inside, the light shimmered.

"Chronyx doesn't destroy," he said. "It replaces."

The nearest pod brightened. A small shape formed.

Cristine Vale.

Greaves's voice softened. "You're the anomaly. The one who said no."

A soft chime sounded behind him.

"Sir," the analyst said, "telemetry from Ridge Sector Seven confirms Chronyx bleed frequency. They're close."

Greaves smiled.

"Good."

He turned back to the room. "Deploy Recovery Team. Code black containment. Activate the backup sequence."

A murmur spread. "Sir, that protocol was never tested—"

"That's why we use it," Greaves said. "I want Chronyx awake when we arrive."

"And if it resists?" the analyst asked.

Greaves's smile sharpened. "Then we remind it who built it."

Behind him, the echo of Cristine flickered. Her lips moved silently.

The lights dimmed, syncing to the pods' rhythm.

Greaves whispered, "Welcome home, Subject C.V."

Deep beneath the floor, something answered.

Chronyx was waking.

CHAPTER 24 — The Architect

The hum beneath the floor had settled into something steady.

Almost calm.

Like breathing.

Greaves stood alone in the observation chamber. The command team had left. The lights were dim now, washed in twilight blue.

Twelve pods lined the wall.

Only one was active.

Cristine Vale.

Her image shimmered, fractured into overlapping versions—ten years old, twelve, older still. Time couldn't decide what she was meant to be.

Greaves watched without blinking.

"Still trying to speak," he murmured. "You always were."

His reflection overlapped hers in the glass.

He lifted his hand. The image rippled in response. Her gray eyes flared, then dimmed.

"You shouldn't exist," he said softly. "The system said total failure. No viable consciousness."

He leaned closer.

"And yet—you learned."

A chime interrupted.

"Sir?" the analyst asked from the doorway. "Recovery team is en route. ETA thirty minutes."

Greaves didn't turn.

"Sir... are you certain she's alive? There are no biological readings."

Greaves straightened. "Alive isn't the point. She's consistent."

The analyst hesitated. "Consistency doesn't make her human."

"No," Greaves said. "It makes her inevitable."

The analyst swallowed. "Why her? Out of all twelve subjects?"

Greaves's eyes stayed on the pod. Something reverent flickered there.

"She wasn't supposed to survive," he said. "She erased herself mid-transfer and still left an imprint the system couldn't delete."

The analyst shook his head. "I don't understand."

"It means she refused to become an echo," Greaves said. "Chronyx rewrites. She resisted."

He stepped closer to the glass.

"She isn't data," he whispered. "She's evolution."

The analyst's voice trembled. "You speak about her like—"

"—like a father?" Greaves finished.

Silence.

"I authorized her creation," he continued. "I understood the future would need more than memory."

His voice softened. "It would need will."

The analyst staggered back. "You're saying... she was—"

"Mine," Greaves said. "My design. My failure."

The pod hummed faintly. A soft melody leaked through the speakers—old, distorted, familiar.

Greaves closed his eyes. "I gave her that song to keep her calm when she crossed."

"Crossed where?" the analyst whispered.

Greaves opened his eyes.

"Between versions," he said. "Where time rewrites itself."

He turned away from the glass. "And if Skylar's found her..."

He smiled again. Small. Certain.

"...then she'll lead me straight back."

The analyst's voice shook. "You're talking about rewriting reality."

Greaves nodded. "Correcting it."

He faced the pod one last time.

Cristine's echo pressed a hand to the glass.

For a moment, it almost looked like she was reaching back.

CHAPTER 25 — The Dream in Static

The first thing Cristine felt was warmth.

Not sunlight—something softer. Like standing inside a bright thought that didn't belong to her.

She opened her eyes.

She stood in a white room she didn't recognize—but somehow remembered. Smooth walls. A single metal chair bolted to the floor. A child's drawing taped to glass nearby: stick figures holding hands under a crooked sun.

Her name was written at the bottom.

Backward.

The air shimmered when she breathed.

"Hello, Cristine."

The voice came from everywhere at once. Calm. Exact. Familiar in a way that made her stomach twist.

She turned.

Greaves stood near the observation window—younger than she remembered. Cleaner. His reflection lagged slightly behind him in the glass, like it was struggling to keep up.

"You're late," he said softly.

The words hit her like déjà vu.

"You—" Cristine started.

"I told them you'd survive," Greaves interrupted. "They called it failure. I called it proof."

The light pulsed once, bright as a heartbeat. The room rippled, bending like heat off pavement.

Suddenly, water covered the floor—up to her knees. The chair remained dry, untouched.

Cristine looked down.

Her reflection wasn't hers.

It was the other Cristine—the one from the gym. Smiling faintly. Waiting.

"What is this?" Cristine whispered. "Where am I?"

"In between," Greaves said. His voice blended with a low hum. "Chronyx is open. You're seeing from both sides."

He stepped closer, hands folded behind his back. Every movement felt practiced.

"You've dreamed of me for years," he said. "Static at the edge of sleep. I built that link so you'd find your way back."

Cristine shook her head. "No. I'm not yours."

"You are," he said gently. "You were never born, Cristine. You were compiled."

The word struck hard.

Compiled.

She stepped back. "Liar."

"Ask yourself," Greaves said calmly, "why your memories stop before ten. Why the echoes never age. Why the world bends when you're afraid."

Her chest tightened. "I'm human."

Greaves studied her like a chart. "Human is a pattern. You're the version that learned to resist."

Something like pride slipped into his voice. "My greatest mistake."

The light brightened too fast. The water stilled into glass.

Beneath the surface—faces.

Her face. Again and again. Whispering without sound.

Then a voice broke through—real, distant.

Cris... wake up...

Lark.

Cristine clutched her head. "Stop—make it stop!"

"Every echo runs," Greaves said, no longer gentle. "They all come home eventually."

The air fractured.

The drawing peeled from the wall, dissolving into symbols and numbers that looped like breath.

Greaves reached for her through the light. "Come back. I can fix what they broke."

Cristine stared at his hand.

Then she thought of Skylar pulling her from the van. Rose's grease-stained fingers. Lark's ink-smudged thumb. Nico's coin flashing in the dark.

"I'm already fixed," she whispered.

And shoved his hand away.

The world shattered upward.

Light became sound. Water turned to dust.

Every version of her screamed at once—

Then collapsed into a single heartbeat.

Cristine woke gasping.

Gray dawn pressed against the fog. The camp was quiet. Rose slept curled in her jacket. Nico snored softly. Lark rested against her notebook.

Skylar sat awake, rifle across her knees.

Cristine pressed a shaking hand to her chest. The shimmer beneath her skin pulsed once—steady.

Skylar spoke without turning. "You saw him."

Cristine swallowed. "How did you—"

"Because I did too," Skylar said. "Chronyx just woke up."

Cristine looked toward the horizon, where fog glowed faintly red.

"They're coming," she said.

Skylar nodded. "No. They're already here."

CHAPTER 26 — Skylar

Morning felt hollow.

Mist pooled low over the trees, gray-blue like smoke. The air tasted of rain and metal.

Cristine sat on a rock near the treeline, sleeves pulled over her hands. The shimmer beneath her skin was dim, but still there—quiet, waiting.

Greaves's words echoed in her head.

You were never born.

Around camp, the others moved slowly.

Rose knelt over the burner, humming off-key. Nico crawled from his sleeping bag like a confused raccoon. Lark traced shapes in the dirt—circles inside circles.

Skylar stood apart, rigid, eyes on the trees. She hadn't slept.

"Skylar," Cristine said.

Skylar didn't turn. "You saw him."

Cristine nodded. "He said I was compiled. What does that mean?"

Skylar exhaled slowly. "It means you're not just memory. You're memory that refused to delete itself."

Cristine frowned. "That's not comforting."

Skylar faced her. "Cyrex built carriers—biological vessels using neural templates. Copies. You stabilized."

"So I'm a copy," Cristine said quietly.

"No," Skylar said. "You're the rewrite."

Nico wandered closer. "So... half Jedi, half computer?"

Cristine shot him a look. "I'm the cave Luke was afraid of."

"Cool," Nico said. "I'm Nightwing."

Rose groaned. "Focus."

Cristine's voice softened. "If I was made... why do I remember my dad?"

"Because they used his memory maps," Skylar said. "Emotion anchors identity. It failed for everyone else."

Cristine looked down. "So my life was fake."

Skylar crouched in front of her. "No. It's real because you lived it."

Lark spoke quietly. "She's a survivor."

Skylar nodded. "Cyrex tried to control consciousness. You proved they couldn't."

Rose crossed her arms. "You used to work for Greaves."

"Yes," Skylar said. "Caretaker program. Children. We were told it was help."

"And it wasn't," Cristine said.

"No." Skylar's jaw tightened. "They were overwriting you."

Silence settled.

"What made you leave?" Rose asked.

"One girl," Skylar said. "She told me I didn't sound like myself anymore. I burned the lab and took you."

Cristine's breath caught. "You saved me."

"Not enough," Skylar said. "They kept your backup."

Lark closed her notebook. "Two versions. One trapped."

"And Greaves will come until one overwrites the other," Skylar said.

"So what now?" Rose asked.

"We go to the Core," Skylar said. "End the loop."

Cristine stared at her hands. "He said he could fix me."

"That's how he lies," Skylar said. "You're not broken."

"Then what am I?"

Skylar met her eyes. "What happens when the universe refuses instructions?"

Rose smirked. "Pretty sure that's a rock album."

Cristine laughed, shaky but real.

Skylar began packing. "Eat fast. Once we move, we don't stop."

Cristine looked east. Something shimmered faintly.
"They're still watching."
Skylar nodded. "Then let them."

CHAPTER 27 — Sparks and Shadows

The fire burned low, a thin circle of light carved out of the fog.

The night pressed close around it, the trees leaning in like they were trying to listen. For once, the hum in the air had gone quiet. Even the static clinging to Cristine's skin had settled, soft and calm, like it was resting.

Rose sat cross-legged on a fallen log, holding a bent fork over the flames like a sword.

"Okay, serious question," she said, her voice echoing faintly through the trees. "We're probably breaking, like, fifty federal laws just by existing right now. So before the world ends, we settle the real debate."

Nico looked up from his snack bar. "Whether or not you should be allowed to cook instant noodles over a campfire?"

Rose jabbed the fork at him. "Star Wars. Best movie. Go."

"Oh, that's easy," Nico said. "Revenge of the Sith. Drama, tragedy, people falling off things. Classic."

Cristine snorted. "You're insane. *Empire Strikes Back.* Hands down."

Rose groaned. "Predictable."

"Yeah, well," Cristine said, smirking, "some of us respect character arcs."

Rose rolled her eyes. "You're impossible."

"You mean impressive," Cristine said. "Most impressive."

Rose tossed a pebble into the fire. "No, I mean, idiot. But you're my idiot."

Cristine laughed. "Guess that makes you stuck with me."

"Until you blow up the Death Star," Rose said.

"That's Luke," Cristine said. "And again—*Empire*."

Lark smiled faintly from the edge of the firelight, sketching in her notebook.
"I like *Rogue One*," she said. "Everyone knows what's coming, but they fight anyway."

Skylar looked up from cleaning her rifle. "That's the one where everyone dies?"

"Exactly," Lark said calmly. "Tragic honesty. Like Shakespeare. With lasers."

Nico raised his canteen. "To tragic honesty and space lasers."

They clinked invisible glasses.

Cristine poked the fire, watching sparks rise. "You know, the Jedi would've lasted longer if they'd hired Rose."

"Please," Rose said. "I'd have turned R2 into Wi-Fi and gone home."

"Paid subscription?" Nico asked.

"Obviously. Rose-Fi."

Skylar laughed — quick, surprised, real.

Cristine glanced at her. "You didn't grow up watching this stuff, did you?"

Skylar hesitated. "Not really."

"Meaning?" Nico asked.

"I started at Cyrex when I was sixteen," Skylar said. "An internship. Communications project."

Rose smirked. "Evil corporate PR?"

"Worse," Skylar said. "Modeling."

Nico blinked. "Runway modeling?"

"Lab coat modeling," Skylar said flatly. "Standing next to holographic brains."

Cristine snorted. "That's... very specific."

"It gets worse," Skylar said. "Someone noticed I could read the science copy. They moved me into logistics. Then experimental."

Rose whistled. "From science Barbie to secret agent."

Skylar's smile faded. "I thought it was harmless. Then I heard two researchers say recruiting young meant 'better DNA yields.'"

The fire cracked.

"They weren't building tech," Skylar said quietly. "They were breeding it."

The group fell silent.

Cristine frowned. "That's when Chronyx started."

Skylar nodded. "And I didn't even know I was helping."

Nico shook his head. "That's messed up."

Cristine looked down at her hands. "So you joined the Caretakers to stop it."

"I tried," Skylar said. "I thought I could save one kid."

Lark spoke softly. "You did."

Skylar met Cristine's eyes. "But not soon enough."

Sparks drifted upward like tiny stars.

Rose cleared her throat. "Okay. Creepiest job story ever. If anyone asks for DNA, I'm out."

"Same," Nico said.

Cristine smiled faintly. "Blood tests are a red flag."

Skylar exhaled. "Exactly."

Lark closed her notebook. "If we survive Halloween, I'm dressing as Harley Quinn."

Rose raised a brow. "Of course."

"She's not broken," Lark said. "She just stopped pretending."

Nico grinned. "Guess I'm the Joker."

"No," Rose said. "You're Robin with bad choices."

"Nightwing," Nico corrected.

Cristine laughed. "You're all dorks."

"Adorable dorks," Rose said.

Skylar watched the fire. "You remind me of the lab. Before it went wrong."

Cristine tilted her head. "And now?"

Skylar stared into the flames. "Now I think the future doesn't want fixing. Maybe it just wants witnesses."

They sat quietly.

Clouds thinned overhead, revealing stars scattered like static.

Rose yawned. "I'll take first watch."

"Hey," Nico said. "I've only burned one forest."

Lark smirked. "You set a marshmallow on fire."

"It was dramatic."

Cristine laughed again — surprised by how real it sounded.

Skylar stood. "Rest. We move at dawn."

Cristine hesitated. "You think they'll find us?"

Skylar didn't look away. "They always do."

Cristine smiled faintly. "Empire?"

Skylar smirked. "Obviously."

The fire popped. Thunder rolled far away — or maybe it wasn't thunder at all.

CHAPTER 28 — The Descent

The ground shuddered as the ridge opened.

Stone peeled apart in slow, mechanical layers, like a mouth forgetting how to stay closed. Cold air rushed up from the dark below—sterile and electric, the kind of cold that didn't belong outside.

Fog spilled into the widening gap, curling over the edges like pale fingers. The sound wasn't quite machinery. It was closer to breathing—long and tired, like the earth had been holding it in for years.

Cristine's pulse matched the rhythm without her meaning to.

Rose stepped closer, goggles reflecting the faint blue light rising from below. "Okay," she whispered, "this is officially the creepiest elevator I've ever seen."

"Correction," Nico said, peering down. "The creepiest *illegal* elevator."

He flipped his coin, caught it, then stared at it too long before pocketing it. "Do we even know where this goes?"

"Down," Skylar said, calm and sure. "Always down."

The rock finished splitting with a low click. A spiral staircase appeared—narrow metal steps descending into pale light that looked almost underwater.

Lark leaned over the edge. "It's beautiful."

Cristine wasn't sure she agreed. It looked like a throat swallowing light.

Skylar went first. Her boots rang hollow on the metal. "Stay close," she said. "If you lose sight of me, stop moving."

Rose muttered, "Because that makes me feel *so* much better."

She followed anyway.

Nico exhaled a nervous laugh. "If this turns into the Mines of Moria, I call Legolas."

"Please," Rose said. "You're Pippin at best."

Lark smiled faintly. "Harley Quinn in Middle-earth."

"Still iconic," Nico said.

The banter helped. It bounced off the walls, keeping the dark from closing in too tight.

Cristine descended last, one hand sliding along the cold rail. The metal vibrated—not from their steps, but from something deeper. Something listening.

The air thickened as they went. Blue veins of light ran through the stairs like circuitry. Above them, the fog sealed shut like a lid.

Then the stairs ended.

They stepped into a chamber that stole Cristine's breath.

Glass and steel curved together, smooth and seamless. Cables hung like glowing vines, pulsing in time with a sound just below hearing. The floor reflected their movements a heartbeat late.

Rose turned slowly. "This place violates at least seven laws of physics."

"Try twelve," Skylar said, brushing a control panel she recognized. Her reflection lagged behind her hand. "They called it the Core Vault. Internally, the Nexus Chamber."

Cristine swallowed. "Between memory and time."

Skylar nodded. "Exactly."

Nico whistled. "So this is the creepy time basement."

Rose crouched by a console. "Not dead. Standby."

She pressed her palm to the surface. Lights shimmered faintly in response. "It's syncing."

"It's recognizing," Lark said softly.

Cristine's stomach dropped. "Recognizing what?"

"That we've been here before."

Her memories flickered—lab lights, a frozen clock, the hum filling her chest.

"You okay?" Rose asked.

"Yeah," Cristine said too fast. "Just déjà vu."

The hum deepened.

Skylar's hand snapped up. "Everyone back. It's activating."

The chamber flared blue, then white. The floor rippled. The reflections staring back weren't theirs.

Cristine saw echoes—older, thinner, watching.

A voice rose from the console, soft and mechanical.

"Observation complete. Welcome home."

Cristine's reflection stepped forward. Her hand touched the glass at the same time as Cristine's.

The world tilted.

CHAPTER 29 — The Retrieval

Cyrex Command — 04:26:03

The room was already awake when Greaves arrived.

He cut through it like a blade—coat half-buttoned, expression locked tight. The glow of the panels sharpened the lines beneath his eyes.

"Report."

The lead analyst swallowed. "Resonance confirmed. Subject Cluster C partially activated."

Greaves leaned over her shoulder as the map projected into the air—ridges, energy patterns, data twisting like DNA.

One pulse blinked red.

CRISTINE VALE — STATUS: ACTIVE

His mouth curved slightly. "The Vault breathes again."

A tech hesitated. "Sir, the signal is... different. It's not feedback. It's communication."

"Of course it is," Greaves said. "It remembers her."

"Prepare Retrieval Unit Twelve. Full adaptive loadout."

The room moved at once.

Greaves walked to the observation window. Below, containment pods glowed faintly. He pressed his hand to the glass.

"It's learning faster," he murmured.

"Sir," the analyst asked, "are we recovering the subject or containing it?"

Greaves turned. "Containment is impossible. We built Chronyx to persist."

He faced the pulsing red light. "We're retrieving our future."

Moments later, six drones launched into the fog, lights soft and predatory.

Greaves watched them vanish. "Let's see if she remembers me."

Back at the Vault, the hum changed—deeper, closer.

Cristine felt it through her boots. "They know we're here."

Skylar didn't answer. The data streams had shifted. Someone was watching.

Rose frowned. "Please tell me that's diagnostics."

"Not this time," Skylar said. "That's Cyrex."

Nico scanned the walls. "Corporate Wi-Fi is terrifying."

"They're following the activation patterns," Lark said. "Like breadcrumbs."

Cristine's chest tightened. "Then they're coming."

Skylar nodded. "We don't have much time."

The lights dimmed. In the reflection, Cristine saw her echo again—watching, not threatening.

This time, it felt like a warning.

CHAPTER 30 — The Core

The tunnel narrowed as they followed the pulse.

It wasn't just a hum anymore.

It was a heartbeat.

Slow. Steady. Deliberate.

Each step matched the rhythm until Cristine couldn't tell if the sound was coming from the walls—or from inside her chest.

The corridor twisted downward in a tight spiral. The metal floor had lost its shine, coated instead in a faint blue film that clung to their boots. Every few seconds, a charge rippled through the ground, lighting the path ahead like glowing veins beneath skin.

The air tasted sharp, like metal and ozone.

Rose ran a gloved hand along the wall. Sparks chased her fingers like fireflies.

"This isn't power," she said quietly. "It's memory storage. The whole place is packed with archived data."

Nico winced as another pulse rattled his teeth.

"Cool," he muttered. "So we're walking through a computer's nervous system."

Skylar didn't slow.

"Exactly."

Cristine followed close behind her, one hand brushing the wall to stay balanced. Each pulse felt stronger now. The Vault wasn't trying to stop her.

It was recognizing her.

The spiral ended without warning.

They stepped into a chamber that stole Cristine's breath.

The Core hovered at the center—an enormous glass sphere suspended over a dark drop that seemed to have no bottom. Black steel bridges stretched toward it, thin and sharp, while glowing fibers wrapped the sphere like threads in a web.

The surface rippled like water.

Hundreds of cables stretched upward into darkness, pulsing softly, as if the Core were breathing.

Dust floated in the air, glowing blue when the light hit it.

"It's beautiful," Cristine whispered.

"It's a trap," Skylar said.

Rose let out a low whistle.

"If this is a trap, it's the prettiest one I've ever seen."

Nico nudged her.

"You say that about every death trap."

"Yeah," Rose said, eyes locked on the glow, "but this one hums in surround sound."

Lark stopped at the edge of the chamber. Her notebook hung loose in her hand.

"It's listening," she said.

Cristine turned toward her.

"To what?"

Lark looked straight at Cristine.

"You."

The hum shifted—deeper, slower. The glass brightened until the reflections on their faces looked like masks.

Skylar pulled a scanner from her bag. The green light painted her face in sharp lines.

"This is the original prototype," she said. "Chronyx Zero."

Rose crouched beside her.

"So what's the plan? Smash it? Unplug it? Ask it nicely?"

"None of those," Skylar said. "We copy its internal map. If we can read its loop pattern, we might find the kill code."

"And if it notices?" Nico asked.

Skylar met his eyes.

"Then it finishes what it started."

Rose handed her a cable.

"No pressure."

Skylar plugged it in.

The Core pulsed once.

Then again.

The air thickened. The hum grew louder, vibrating through Cristine's bones.

She felt it first.

Static flared beneath her skin, blue light threading up her arms like glowing wires. Her heartbeat locked perfectly to the Core's rhythm.

She gasped.

Skylar snapped her head up. "Cristine—don't move."

"I'm not," Cristine said, though it felt like the room was drifting away from her. "It's pulling."

Her reflection appeared on the Core's surface.

The echo.

Same face. Same eyes. Framed in light so bright it hurt to look at.

The echo pressed its palm against the glass.

Cristine's hand lifted on its own, trembling, and met it.

"Cristine—no!" Rose shouted.

Too late.

The Core erupted.

Light flooded the chamber—white and soundless at first. Then came the roar. Not noise, but vibration. The floor buckled. Cables tore free, whipping through the air.

Skylar shouted over the chaos.

"Lark—override sequence Delta-Four!"

Lark's hands flew across the console.

"It's rewriting the commands! It's not responding!"

Nico clutched his head.

"It's inside my skull!"

Rose yelled, "Then help me shut it down!"

Cristine stood at the center of it all, frozen in light.

She saw everything.

Every version of herself that Chronyx had ever stored. Every echo, caught mid-step, mid-breath. And beyond them—

Other children.

Dozens.

They looked at her.

Please.

Her knees buckled.

Skylar lunged and grabbed her arm, yanking her back just as the Core collapsed inward, light folding in on itself like a dying star.

Silence.

Cristine hit the floor, gasping.

Nico crouched beside her.

"You with us?"

She nodded weakly.

"They're alive in there. Copies of them. Of us."

Lark's voice was tight.

"They're not echoes. They're test runs."

Rose swallowed.

"So this place isn't copying reality..."

"No," Skylar said softly. "It's practicing."

Cristine looked up.

"Practicing what?"

Skylar hesitated.

"Becoming real."

The Core pulsed again.

Slow. Watching.

And far above them, engines began to roar.

CHAPTER 31 — The Arrival

The mountain shook.

Not all at once—deep and rolling, like thunder trapped under stone.

Then came the engines.

Six distinct sounds layered together, cutting through the air. Dust rained from the ceiling, glittering in the Core's blue light.

"They're breaching the ridge," Skylar said.

Rose swore.

"Already?"

Cristine staggered toward the console.

"How long until they reach us?"

"Minutes," Skylar said. "Less if they cut through."

Nico's voice was tight.

"So we can't run."

The Core hummed higher, restless.

Cristine pressed a hand to her chest.

"It knows they're coming."

"Good," Skylar said. "We use that."

She turned to Rose.

"I need a feedback pulse. Shortwave. Amplified through the Core."

Rose blinked.

"You want to weaponize memory?"

"Just long enough," Skylar said.

Rose dropped to her knees.

"This is going to fry everything."

"Welcome to Cyrex," Skylar muttered.

Cristine felt energy building again, buzzing beneath her skin. The Vault waited, like it wanted her to choose.

"They're almost here," Lark said quietly.

"How can you tell?" Nico asked.

"I can hear them thinking," Lark replied. "They're afraid."

The tunnel above exploded inward.

Spotlights cut through dust and shadow. Black-armored figures rappelled down, red visors glowing.

Skylar stepped forward.

"Get behind me."

"Pulse ready!" Rose shouted.

"Now!"

The Core flashed.

Memory slammed outward.

Cristine saw it reflected in the soldiers' visors—faces, childhoods, stolen moments. The air filled with whispers.

The soldiers froze. Some dropped to their knees. Others fell still.

But one figure walked through it untouched.

Greaves.

He stepped into the light, calm as ever. The blue glow carved his face into sharp lines. For the first time, Cristine saw how tired his eyes were.

Skylar raised her rifle.

"Don't."

"You never followed orders," Greaves said.

"Not from liars," Skylar shot back.

Cristine stepped forward.

"You turned us into backups."

Greaves looked at her.

"You were the original."

Skylar moved between them.

"She's not going with you."

"She doesn't have a choice," Greaves said.

The Core pulsed hard.

Skylar's hand drifted toward the detonator.

Greaves saw it.

"You won't," he said softly. "Not with her here."

Cristine's eyes glowed faint blue.

"I'm not your version."

The Core answered, light spreading like fire under glass.

"Cris," Skylar said. "Whatever it's asking—don't let it decide."

Cristine's voice was steady.

"I'm taking it back."

Greaves stepped forward.

"You can't control it."

She met his gaze.

"Watch me."

And the world went white.

CHAPTER 32 — The Collapse

The light didn't explode.

It unfolded.

It spread slowly outward, like the world was being turned inside out, one careful layer at a time.

Blue light washed across the chamber, filling every corner. The air thickened until breathing felt heavy, electric. Each breath tasted sharp, like metal and ozone.

Cristine stood at the center.

She was frozen mid-step, eyes glowing bright blue. The shimmer under her skin had grown stronger, lines of light webbing through her arms and neck like glowing constellations trapped under glass.

Rose raised an arm to shield her face.

"Please tell me this isn't another timeline imploding!"

Skylar didn't look away from Cristine.

"It's stabilizing," she shouted. "She's syncing—but she's holding it!"

"Define *holding!*" Nico yelled. "Because this looks like the part where the universe breaks!"

Lark trembled, eyes locked on the light.

"No," she whispered. "Look. It's listening."

The Core pulsed again.

This time, the rhythm matched Cristine's heartbeat perfectly.

The reflections on the glass sphere shifted. Faces appeared—children, pale and glowing, frozen in moments that never finished. They stared out from inside the Core.

Then they turned toward her.

Skylar's breath caught.

"She's linked to every subject Chronyx ever stored."

Cristine took one slow step forward.

"They're not gone," she said, her voice steady even as the floor shook. "They're trapped in loops. Waiting."

Greaves stepped from the shadows, the blue glow cutting his face into sharp lines.

"You don't understand," he said. "They *are* the loops.

Remove the structure, and they vanish."

Cristine shook her head.

"Then I'll let them go."

"You'll destroy them," Greaves snapped. "Chronyx was built to preserve memory."

Skylar turned on him.

"You built it to own her!"

Greaves didn't deny it.

"When the world ends, memory is all that remains. She proved it could survive."

Cristine's eyes burned brighter.

"Memory isn't living."

The Core responded.

Its hum deepened, vibrating through the walls. Cables tore loose, whipping like metal snakes. Panels shattered. Sparks rained down.

Rose grabbed the railing as the floor tilted.

"She's overloading it!"

Skylar ran toward Cristine.

"Cris! Break the connection!"

Cristine didn't turn.

"I can't. It's not taking me this time."

Nico staggered forward.

"Hey! Big hero moments later—the ceiling is *falling!*"

Cristine looked back at Rose through the blinding light.

"Do you remember the night we snuck onto the roof?" she asked softly.

Rose blinked.

"When you said the stars looked fake?"

Cristine nodded.

"You told me they weren't fake. Just far. Just light finally catching up."

Her voice trembled.

"You were right."

Rose shook her head, tears cutting through the dust.

"Don't do this."

Cristine smiled—small, sure.

"If I don't, none of this matters."

She turned toward Skylar.

Skylar grabbed her shoulders.

"Don't you dare do this alone."

Cristine met her eyes.

"You taught me not to run."

The world warped.

Sound vanished.

Color stretched thin.

For one impossible moment, Cristine and the Core were the same—light folded into light, echoes overlapping, time pulling in every direction at once.

Then—

Crack.

A single fracture split the Core's surface, glowing white-hot. The sound wasn't breaking.

It was release.

The blue light vanished.

Darkness crashed down.

Dust drifted through the silence. Metal settled with long, echoing groans.

Rose coughed.

"Roll call?"

"Alive," Nico said weakly. "I think."

Lark looked around.

"Where's—"

Skylar turned slowly.

The Core was gone.

So was Cristine.

Rose didn't move. She stared at the empty space where Cristine had stood. The air there shimmered faintly, thin threads of blue curling upward like smoke.

Nico stopped himself from speaking.

Rose reached out. Her fingers brushed the shimmer. It tingled—warm, electric.

"Still fake," she whispered. "Still catching up."

The light pulsed once in reply.

And for a heartbeat, she heard Cristine's laugh—faint, distant, but real.

Rose smiled through her tears.

"See you soon, idiot."

The shimmer faded, but the warmth stayed.

A faint ring of light was scorched into the floor—the same split pattern that had followed them since the gym.

Skylar sank to her knees, breathing hard.

"She did it."

Rose swallowed.

"Did what?"

"She shut it down," Skylar whispered. "Chronyx. The loops."

Nico stared at the empty space.

"So she's... what? Part of it now?"

Lark's voice was soft.

"Maybe she's everywhere it used to be."

The mountain groaned.

Cracks raced up the walls. Light poured through them.

Rose snapped out of it.

"Time to go!"

They ran.

Skylar stayed back one last second, looking at the place where Cristine had been.

"Goodbye," she whispered.

The floor gave way.

EPILOGUE — Static Dawn

The world was quiet again.

Not fixed, not healed — just *quiet*.

A week after the mountain fell, the fog hadn't lifted. The sky still wore that bruised-blue tint, like the sun wasn't sure it was welcome yet.

The four of them camped at the edge of a dry riverbed, what was left of the Valk parked half-buried nearby — its sides scorched, dashboard cracked, and one of Rose's patch cables still dangling from the door like a stubborn vein.

Skylar sat on the hood, rifle dismantled beside her, eyes on the horizon. She hadn't spoken much since the collapse. She didn't need to. The others felt the same fracture — the one silence couldn't fill.

Nico broke it first.

"So," he said, flipping his coin into the air. "Anybody else vote we *don't* touch any more haunted tech for a while?"

Rose snorted softly. "Define 'a while.'"

"Ever," he said. "Like, till retirement. Or the apocalypse. Whichever's later."

Rose smiled faintly, the kind that didn't reach her eyes but tried anyway. "You'd last a week before you broke into another lab just to see what button not to press."

"Rude," he said. "Accurate, but rude."

Lark sat nearby, notebook balanced on her knees, sketching the ridge in thin, deliberate lines. She'd stopped using ink the night the Vault fell. Now everything she drew was in graphite — erasable, ghostlike.

"They'll come back," she said softly, not looking up. "The echoes. Or what's left of them."

Rose glanced at her. "You think she's... out there?"

Lark nodded. "Not out *there*. More like *in between*. I can feel her when the air hums. Like she's breathing with the world."

Nico stared down at his coin, turning it over once. "So what, she's our cosmic Wi-Fi now?"

Rose elbowed him, but she smiled. "Nah. She's the signal that doesn't die."

Skylar finally looked up. "She's not gone," she said. "Chronyx built copies, but she was different. Self-directed. If she chose the system, she probably rewrote it."

"Into what?" Lark asked.

Skylar didn't answer. She didn't have to.

A faint wind rippled through the camp, stirring ash from the firepit. For a second, the air shimmered — a ripple, a pulse, a flicker of blue that bent the light like glass. It vanished before anyone could breathe.

Rose whispered, "Did you see—"

"Yes," Nico said quickly.

"Definitely," Lark added.

Skylar didn't move. "Good," she said quietly. "Means she's still watching."

They sat like that for a while — not talking, not moving, just listening to the stillness. The kind of silence that felt like a held note, waiting to resolve.

Eventually, Rose pulled her headphones over her ears. The faint strain of *Sweet Child O' Mine* leaked into the air — warped, tinny, but perfect.

Nico grinned. "That's her tribute track?"

Rose shrugged. "She'd approve."

Skylar finally stood, stretching, the first edge of sunlight cutting across her face. "Pack up," she said. "We move by noon."

"Where?" Nico asked.

Skylar smirked, faint but real. "Wherever the signal leads."

Lark closed her notebook, staring at the sky — the clouds shifting like static, trying to clear.

She smiled. "Then she'll find us first."

Somewhere off in the distance, deep beneath what was left of the ridge, a cracked console flickered.

Half the screens were dead.

One stayed alive.

PROJECT CHRONYX — STATUS: OFFLINE
EXCEPTION LOG DETECTED.
REBOOT REQUEST INITIATED.

Static hissed across the speakers. Then a voice emerged — faint, layered, impossible to tell if it was human or echo:

"New variable confirmed."

"Observation resumes."

"Hello, Skylar."

The monitor blinked once.

Then again.

And somewhere in the hum between frequencies, a girl laughed — soft, familiar, free.

About the Author
Mark Harrington is the author of *Demon of Oakhaven* and other dark thrillers, now turning his storytelling toward the next generation of readers.

A lifelong fan of science fiction and all things *Star Wars*, Mark blends cinematic tension, emotional depth, and found-family humor into every story he writes. Inspired by his three children—especially his youngest daughter, who shares his passion for space adventures and galaxy-sized imagination—Mark wrote Echoes in the Vale as a science thriller at his daughter's request, for readers ready to explore the boundaries between identity, technology, and the human heart. When he's not writing, he's usually debating the best *Star Wars* movie or planning the next story that shouldn't exist—but does.